HB
The Getaway
Chapter 5

Cyd Webster

ISBN: 0989280500
ISBN-13: 978-0-9892805-0-1

DEDICATION

I dedicate this book to my beautiful nieces Keturah Webster and Jade Webster and step-granddaughter, Brittni Duhart. My prayer is that you continue to be strong, proud, wise, and know that you are wonderfully made.

HB - THE GETAWAY
CHAPTER 5
Main Characters

Annelle Carter - Annelle is the protagonist of the story who is a very intelligent microbiophysicist, born and raised in Orange, New Jersey. She studied at The Ohio State University, graduating with a PhD by the age of 24. She subsequently went to work for a company called Nibiodymics in Toledo, Ohio. After the catastrophic, nuclear event, she moved into the 'safe zone' in Hammond, Indiana and continued to work for Nibiodymics as the creator of the HB android.

Janice - Janice grew up in Orange, NJ and is Annelle's best friend. She has known Annelle and her family most of her life. Janice moved to Hammond, IN, following Annelle and eventually purchased an HB, Ronald.

Stacey - Stacey is longtime friend of Annelle and Janice who grew up in Orange, NJ. She moved to Atlanta but eventually moved in with Annelle in Hammond. Stacey is totally against the creation of the HB android.

Sheila - Sheila met Annelle at the retreat at a spa resort that the ladies visited. She was invited by Annelle's cousin Patlyn. Sheila lives in Detroit and won an HB in a contest.

Patlyn - Patlyn is Annelle's cousin who moved from Detroit to Toronto, Ontario after the nuclear event. She brought Sheila with her to the 'get-away' retreat.

Candace - Candace is Stacey's friend from Atlanta. She joined the ladies for the 'get-away' retreat.

ACKNOWLEDGMENTS

I thank our most loving and merciful God for providing opportunities and allowing me the wisdom to pursue them. I am so grateful for my family and friends... especially my good friends who have been so supportive of my efforts. Thank you Kareemah Rogers, for inspiration and for providing the venue to promote HB Chapter 5 at your Sisters Soup and Sentiment party. Thank you Doreen Adams for your eagerness and persistence, you are a true accountability partner. Thank you Shirley Hendricks, Sharon Jones, Lois Robinson, June Morgan, Cynthia Miller, Evelyn Barrios, my sister Carla Miller, and so many others who have encouraged and inspired me. A special thanks to my husband, George Beacham... I love you for making me feel so special. Your encouragement keeps me motivated and I am so blessed to have you in my life.

1 THE GETAWAY

"Come on up here Annelle! We have to get you packed! I promised Janice that I'd get you all packed up and off to the airport tomorrow."

"OK, here I come" Annelle yelled up to Bruce.

She stood up and gathered all of those old documents that had fallen out of her small suitcase, and packed them back into it. She picked up her garment bag and headed for the stairs, but turned and stared at that suitcase with those documents in it for a few more moments. She felt tense and exhausted at the same time after reflecting on losing Ted and her baby. She knew she needed to get away with friends and was so glad that Bruce was there with her to help her pack. She needed some new air space around her, new scenery- she knew it even more as she stared at that suit case because she wanted to feel better and just seeing all those documents brought back the shock and disbelief that she had been terminated from her job, on top of everything else.

Walter was complicit in the cover-up because he had a huge vested interest in keeping HBs on the market. Annelle was also very upset that Walter had turned his back on her. She felt as if she was stupid or gullible for not realizing the kind of person Walter really was. She was glad that she had stock in the company and her patent would always keep the royalties coming in but she had hoped to take HBs in a new direction after what happened to her. She had been listening to some of the critics and their reasoning behind being so against the idea of HBs, but before what happened with Ted, she was totally focused on the need that she felt that her company fulfilled, successfully. She was torn about the moral and ethical reasons that caused some people to be against HBs all along deep down inside. Yet the disaster with Ted pushed her right over to the other side of the equation. And now she sometimes regrets the way she went about trying to change the focus of their efforts with HBs and Walter

1

simply wasn't having it. It wasn't long after she returned to work that she began presenting proposals for a new direction. Janice and Bruce were both annoyed with her for even working on it while she was in the hospital after losing her baby. They thought she had lost her mind because she didn't even seem to grieve, but became totally immersed in changing direction with HBs and even acted excited about it. She decided that HBs should not be made to replace men as 'head of household, husbands', but as some kind of butler, maid, and home assistants. The sexual aspect of the HBs should be totally eliminated, according to her new plan. And it was that new planning that she was working on, that caused her to be brought to a boardroom and presented with a package that included papers that they wanted her to sign regarding intellectual propriety and disclosure. Annelle was shocked and didn't even see it coming, although Bruce had warned her that they would probably, eventually fire her. Even though she had come to believe in the back of her mind that they might try to terminate her, she had not truly believed it could be a reality. She just couldn't believe that they could run the operation without her, but she was wrong. Walter showed up to that last meeting she had there with two lawyers and their Human Resources VP. She just could not believe they would do it... after all; it was she who brought the HB idea to life for them from the beginning.

She didn't sign anything right away since it was only a little over a month since the Ted incident happened. She had felt that she had regained her composure pretty well, even after losing the baby. But when those papers were presented to her, she knew she had to leave the office and call someone. She had become so tense in that boardroom by trying to keep her composure, that once she got into her car, the relaxation of her muscles caused a small trickle of pee to escape, which jolted her into controlling those muscles and drawing her knees together to stop from wetting her clothes and the car seat. She drove home while making a call to Janice, and then Janice made a call to an attorney for her. Janice arrived at Annelle's house almost at the same time Annelle got there and told Annelle to call her office and let Walter know that she planned to have an attorney review the documentation. Annelle left a message for Walter and wasn't surprised that he didn't answer when she called him because he had begun to avoid her after what happened with Ted. One of the company attorneys actually returned her call and told her that it was a good idea that she have it reviewed by her own attorney, and that they were expecting an answer from her in one week. In the end after some discussion with her attorney, Bruce, and Janice, she accepted the terms of her termination which included her continued support through their Family Planning Center counselors since she had lost the baby.

With an audible sigh, Annelle exhaled and gathered the garment bag in her arms, turned and walked up the stairs into her living room and saw that

Bruce was heading down the stairs from her bedroom.

"I was just about to come down there and get you. What the heck were you doing down there?"

"I had to pick up all those papers you spilled… Are you hungry?"

"Forget about that for now, let's get you packed, and then I'll take you out for something to eat."

Annelle began pulling some of her favorite outfits from the back of her closet because the weather would be a little warmer in Red Rock Canyon than it was in Hammond. It was already getting a little cooler as fall approached toward the end of September and she hadn't taken a vacation like this in years, so she decided that this would be a perfect reason to wear some of the outfits she hadn't had a chance to put on over the summer.

"Annelle, what the heck is this 'mu-mu' looking thing?" Bruce picked up one of the dresses she had tossed from the closet that landed on the bed.

"That's my sun dress! I'm going to lounge around at least one of the days while I'm there…"

"Oh. I'm thinking that I might have to take you shopping when you get back."

Annelle laughed and in the back of her mind, always felt that there was something feminine about Bruce, but she loved him as one of her best friends, and didn't care if he was gay or not. She had decided that he is just one of those kind of effeminate dudes because he does date women and gets into relationships or at least says he wants to.

"Shoes! I forgot to pack my shoes, sneakers, sandals. Oh… and I have to figure out what I'm gonna wear to the airport tomorrow."

"Let's see… Hmmm…" Bruce started rummaging through the boxes of shoes she had stacked in her closet. "Take these two pairs of sandals, and take these sneakers. Oh and take a pair of heels too because y'all might want to dress up one night."

"You're right. Throw them in there. I can wear them with that black dress that I packed."

Bruce brought the shoes out the closet and began wedging them into the already filled suitcase. "OK! I've finally got this gigantic bag closed. You're going to have to pay for the overweight bag you know…"

"Yeah, I know but I just don't want to bother trying to maneuver more than one bag. I'll take my garment bag onto the plane since it folds up so nicely."

"What's that bag you're packing now?"

"That's my purse, silly!"

"What? That ain't no purse! Your laptop is in there!"

"Now Bruce, you know I'm not cutting myself off that way… I have to bring my laptop."

"You promised that you wouldn't do any work while you're away. I'm going to call you and Janice while you're there just to make sure you remember that!"

"Oh Bruce… I'm not going to do any work… I promise. I do plan to write in my journal though… and I need my laptop so I can stay up on current events."

"Well… OK. But, no work! I know your wheels are turning on how to reinvent your idea and you'll have plenty of time to deal with that when you get back."

"You're right. I'm looking forward to this break… I really am!" Annelle laughed because she knew Bruce knew her well enough to know that she will be tempted to work on etching out a new direction for HBs. She continued to pack her carry-on to include her laptop and portfolio, as well as a small purse that fit inside of it. They took her suitcase and garment bag down to the living room and Bruce headed for the door so that he could put her luggage in his car.

"Where are you going?"

"I want to have your luggage in my car so that in the morning all you need to do is get dressed and come on out. I was thinking about spending the night…"

"I'm calling an airport limo. I really appreciate you, Bruce… all you do for me. But I am not going to inconvenience you like that. You're welcome to spend the night though; you can sleep in the other bedroom."

"OK… But let's call the airport limo right now, before we go to dinner."

Bruce made the call and then left her luggage in the foyer near her front door so that when the airport limo came to pick her up in the morning, the driver could grab them and bring them out. They left and went to a local restaurant and both of them decided to have a glass of Shiraz.

"Wow. I am finally feeling like I'm going on vacation. I'm so glad you helped convince me to go. I feel relief already!"

"Well we knew that you needed to get away, not just away from working, but away. New scenery, change in the environment around you is something that everyone needs from time to time."

"Yeah, and I know that. Oh hey… I've been meaning to ask you, how's your sister doing? Did she get settled in after you helped her get into that program?"

"Yeah… I got her in, finally. She gets on my nerves so bad. I just wish she'd get her damn life together. I had told her after the last time she found herself on the street I was done. But I had to help her this time because I knew she actually believed that the man, who took her in 'this time', was going to be the one, which is how she referred to him. Ugh! Celine is just going to make me crazy. I knew that man was no good, the minute I met him, and she had finally stopped using drugs so how in the hell did she think she'd stay clean when that man was selling drugs!"

"What? You didn't tell me he was a drug dealer!"

"I didn't know it myself. They hid that from me for quite a while, until she couldn't hide it anymore. When she stopped answering my phone calls, I had a feeling something was wrong. And then when I finally heard from her, she was asking me for money."

"Oh wow Bruce. I am so sorry... It's a real shame that she can't seem to pull herself up out of the bowels of society."

"Well, it's not easy you know. She didn't have my parents the way I did growing up. It has just been me and her mostly because my brother won't deal with her at all. Sometimes I feel like she'd be better off with an HB at the rate she's going... Whoops... I didn't even mean to bring that up..."

"Oh it's OK Bruce. I'm fine..."

"No, I mean I just didn't want our conversation to turn into a spec and analysis session about those damn HBs. I know your wheels never stop turning about changes you plan to somehow make. Have you spoken to Walter about any of that yet?"

"No, I'm planning to work with another company, but I have to be careful because you know, all those papers I signed, I need to see a lawyer so that I'm not opening myself up to a lawsuit. I have given up dealing with Walter because I just cannot believe how he has turned on me the way he did. I'm still working on my own investigation because I'm just not comfortable with their explanation on what went wrong. It just seemed too deliberate that he..."

"I know, I know... let's not go down this path again. You're going on vacation, remember?"

"Yeah! OK, let's order some food, I'm starved."

Annelle laughed at Bruce stopping her in her tracks from where that conversation was headed because he knew that once she got wound up into it there was no turning back until she had exhausted herself in trying to analyze all kinds of angles as to why Ted tried to kill her. She never believed that he was trying to do some kind of diagnostic of the pregnancy the way she was told by Walter and the technicians and she was disgusted that they tried to convince her as such.

Once they arrived back at Annelle's house, Bruce asked Annelle if she wanted him to stay over that night, but she declined, especially after he kept complaining about sleeping in 'Ted's old room.

"But wouldn't you like to feel the warmth of a real man next to you for a change?"

Annelle laughed and slapped him on the shoulder and pushed him toward his car. "No... you just go on home, Bruce. I love you. Thanks for everything."

"I'll call you in the morning"

"OK. Good night".

The next morning, Annelle woke up before her alarm went off and bounced out the bed with renewed vigor feeling like a well needed vacation was finally under way. The limo arrived and the driver came up to her door as soon as she opened it to get her bags. Right at that moment she felt like her entire body was smiling. She felt so happy to be actually getting away to meet up with friends at a spa resort. She began to pray to herself as she settled back into the leather seat of the limo while the driver pulled off and headed for the highway...

Thank you, Lord, God, Creator of all things. Thank you for keeping me sane and safe throughout all these years. Thank you for giving me such great parents and although they're no longer here, I thank you for blessing me with them for the time we were together. And thank you God for giving me the strength to keep pushing forward, amidst all that I've been through and helping me see the bright side of life rather than focusing on what I feel I have lost. Thank you for my therapist who is an angel that you have put in my path, who has encouraged me to choose happiness as my deliberate choice. And thank you for my angels, Bruce and Janice...

"How's the temperature, ma'am?"

"Oh, it's fine, thank you." Annelle opened her eyes after the driver interrupted her prayer and said audibly, "Amen", and then she gazed out of the window at the fields that were finally growing more green, lately. Over the years, land that had been so strangely affected by the climate that had changed so drastically after the nuclear event back in 2011 was healing itself, it seemed. There were some efforts to replenish the soil with nutrients and that probably did help, but things that used to grow green, had turned to a beautiful orange with lawns of orange velvet grass. It really looked weird, and actually made some people crazy; including Annelle... at least she thought she was going crazy for a short while. She kept thinking she was on another planet, and she wasn't alone. There were some people who still believed they were somehow transported to another planet, and some cults perpetuated the idea. There were also some trees that grew purple and lavender leaves and over the years, they were also becoming 'greener' slowly and gradually, as time went on. Annelle sat back and relaxed thinking about how much things had changed in ten years since the nuclear event. She laid her head back on the seat and for the duration of her ride to the airport, began to think about the different activities she planned to engage in once she arrived in Red Rock Canyon.

As usual, there was a long line at the check in counter because of people like Annelle, who always checked their luggage. She hated people who dragged their huge bags onto the plane, taking up all the space in the overhead compartments, which had become a problem ever since airlines began charging people for the weight and number of their bags that were being checked. She was amazed that this check in process hadn't improved much over the years, other than being able to get boarding passes at home. She loved that part because there were even lines at the kiosks to get them printed at the airport. She never bothered with the sky jacks outside because she had enough experience of them not getting her luggage on her flight. She knew there was a better chance of her luggage making it onto her flight if she dragged her luggage up to the check in counter herself. Once she got all that taken care of, she headed for the lines that were forming for security checks. She hurried down the escalator to take her place in line.

"Shoes off, take your laptops out of your bag, outer jackets off, place any metal objects in the bins provided, no liquids..."

The TSA person standing at the end of the conveyor belt droned on with her instructions as people were already used to this routine pretty much. However, there always seemed to be someone who just had to disrupt the flow by trying to object to the process. *So stupid,* Annelle thought as she watched this man complain that he shouldn't have to take his laptop out since he bought some special carryon bag that was specifically made so that he wouldn't have to. The TSA woman wouldn't hear his argument, and once he refused after she asked him to take it out the second time, she called security and two other TSA men came to get him, take him out of line over to where they were sure to piss this man off even more as they manually went through all of his things. People in line chuckled at how ridiculous this man's protest was, because had he only taken his laptop out as he was asked, he'd have been walking on down to his gate by now. Annelle was perplexed at such a curious thing where people think they have control when they don't, but still decide to take the hard road instead of just getting past the obstacle. As she stood there in line watching that madness, she just shook her head because the man was right about his special bag, but clearly, TSA in the particular airport they were leaving from was not honoring that.

She finally made it through and decided to buy a cup of coffee and find a seat near her gate. Once she sat down, she looked around and tried to decide whether she should take her laptop out or the book she wanted to finish reading. She sat there for a while observing people as they walked by and got stuck on an old woman who reminded her of a cartoon. She literally looked like an animation, among real flesh folks. This woman had pale skin, so pale that it was an odd pink color. But the pinkish hue was probably due to the loud, bright pink rouge she had smeared on her cheeks. She had 'up-swept' her dyed, straw colored blonde hair into a 'French Roll' on the back of her head. Her hair was 'poofed' up on the top and teased around in a kind of wiry nest. She had drawn her eyebrows on and had actually outlined them with a brown pencil. But it was her lips that were so remarkably odd because she had literally drew them onto her face where she wished her lips would be. It forced Annelle to notice that the problem was that she had no lips, and so she took the lipstick and drew outside of the slit of her mouth, an upper lip and made points as if to draw a pucker. And she covered her bottom lip outside from where her slit of a lip ended and it looked so funny. Annelle sat there transfixed on the cartoon woman and wondered how in the world someone could decide that look was in any way normal or nice. The woman had skin hanging from her chin, giving her the look that her head was sitting on her chest, no neck.

"You look familiar... do I know you?" The woman noticed Annelle staring at her, which made Annelle feel the heat of embarrassment expand in her body, and she tried to conceal it.

"Oh! Uh... I was thinking the same thing... do you live in Hammond?"

"No, but you do look familiar. I'm flying out to see my son and his family in Phoenix. They're trying to get me to live there, but I don't like it out west... Oh we're getting ready to board. I hope the plane isn't full, I have an aisle seat and I hate to be crowded when someone has to sit in the middle."

With that, the woman got up and walked up to the line to get on the plane. Annelle chuckled to herself for getting caught staring at the odd looking woman. *I'll bet she's a real piece of work,* she thought to herself as she gathered her things and pulled her boarding pass out. As Annelle stepped up to get her boarding pass scanned, she saw the little old odd woman was standing on the side because she had tried to get on the plan before her zone was called. Annelle tried not to look at her but wasn't successful, and the woman grimaced when she caught Annelle's eye, and said that she thought her zone had been called. Annelle just smiled and walked on into the plane, found the window seat she had requested, placed her book in the seat pocket in front of her, buckled her seat belt and let out a sigh. She couldn't wait for this part of the trip to be over... the process of getting there.

The flight was uneventful, and then finally she arrived in Nevada, which was one of the few places that had preserved its beauty and ambience in the North American Union. Janice had convinced her that she needed a retreat from everything familiar and since she had always wanted to go there, now was just as good a time as any. Even though Annelle knew Janice was right, she had been reluctant to leave the familiar anxiety of her surroundings as if she found some comfort in the familiarity of it. Yet she knew that wasn't healthy and still it was hard to make the effort to tear herself away, making every excuse she could think of why she shouldn't take a vacation at that time. When she tried to find a reason to worry about spending the money to go since she was unemployed, she knew she could afford it and Bruce reminded her of that fact. Besides, she had put some money away for a rainy day, and she had sat in that coffee shop for many, many days, pondering on whether this situation in her life constituted a rainy day. Now that she was finally on her way, she had completely justified the trip as something physically and spiritually necessary, and with the help of Bruce, she arrived at that answer at the last minute and committed to it. They all decided to meet at the spa since each of them were coming from different parts of the country or needed to leave at different times. Annelle got out of the airport shuttle that brought her to the spa resort and was met by the bellman who so graciously greeted her, and began to load her luggage onto the cart. She stood in the entrance way and turned to gaze at the beautiful landscape of sculptured mountains of so many colors. She took in a deep breath, and let it out as she felt further relaxation and serenity begin to seep into her spirit. As she entered the lobby to check in, she spotted Janice who was standing in the middle of the lobby, chatting with Annelle's cousin, Patlyn and two other women.

"Janice" she yelled as she ran toward them.

"Ohhhh you made it! Well I knew you'd get on the plane because Bruce told me he called you while you were at the airport this morning. Gurrrl, I'm so glad you're here. We are going to have a ball!"

They all hugged and then Annelle's cousin Patlyn introduced her friend Sheila to Annelle. Patlyn had moved to an area near Toronto, Ontario and her friend Sheila lived in Detroit, where Patlyn used to live. Janice flew to the spa the day before the others arrived because she wanted to scope the place out and set up an agenda for them, doing some of the legwork with a few suggestions and options that they might want to engage in. She was complaining about their friend Stacey who was supposed to have met her there the day before, but missed her flight, as usual. Annelle laughed as was not surprised that Stacey wasn't there yet. As Annelle turned to go to the desk to check in, Janice grabbed her arm…

"Annelle, this is Candace, Stacey's friend. She ended up leaving Stacey because well, you already know."

"Right!" Annelle laughed, "So what else is new… although, a day late is breaking a new record for her." They all laughed as Candace went on to say, "I told Stacey that I was leaving for the airport at 2:00 pm yesterday and she complained, because you know she likes to make sure she's rushin'. Just wouldn't be right if things went smooth."

Annelle laughed, "I know girl! You had to leave her, but at least she told you to go ahead to the airport instead of having you go to her house expecting you to wait til she got ready".

Shaking her head, Annelle again, turned to go to the desk to check in when Janice grabbed her again and said,

"I ain't thinking about Stacey, Annelle. She missed her flight and you know how hard it is to fly standby these days. She's en route, so I know she'll be here eventually. She couldn't get a direct flight so the last call I got from her she was in Kansas. Whatever. You're already checked in and here's your key to our room. Come on so I can show you where it is" and Janice handed a key card to Annelle, anxious to show her around the beautiful spa resort.

Janice asked Patlyn, Sheila and Candace to meet them at one of the hotel restaurants in an hour so they could have lunch together, and she led Annelle to the elevator while explaining where some of the amenities are in the hotel.

"The fitness center is real nice. I went there this morning, and then took a swim."

"Oh I can't wait, Janice. That's exactly what I plan to do tomorrow morning. I've been looking over some of the activities…"

"Great but wait until you see what I have lined up before you make any decisions… I think you'll like my agenda".

"I know I probably will and I am so glad you came early and did that for us. You're so good at that anyway."

"Candace was so mad when she got here. I couldn't help but laugh and she lightened up after we let her rant for a few minutes. She said that Stacey was determined not to get to that airport early. But you know how we are" Janice chuckled.

"Yep. I still stick to the three hour rule… and that's why I always leave my house three hours early. After the hour drive to get to the airport, I like having around two hours to get through checking in and security so I can get to the gate and relax."

"Yep! I bring a book or magazine and grab a coffee or something and sit back. I ain't into rushing either. Too much stress".

They stepped off the elevator and their room was not far down the hall. Annelle tried her key to make sure it was still magnetized and worked and when the door opened she stepped into a huge beautiful room with a magnificent view of the red rock, mountainous landscape that took her breath away. She walked over to the panoramic windows that were from the floor to the ceiling and stood there and was so awed by it, she wanted to cry tears. "It's so beautiful, isn't it?"

Janice stood there alongside of Annelle and gazed at the natural beauty of the landscape. "It leaves me speechless. God so loved this world… this world that is so undeserving of grace, and yet we are reminded in such a beautiful way of the tremendous love that God has for us."

Annelle then turned to Janice with tears running down her face and Janice gave her a hug and they both cried as Janice began to pray…

"Lord God and creator of all things, please grant us serenity and peace as we make the effort to enjoy ourselves and each other for a glorious retreat in a land that you have spared with beauty and amazing grace. We are so grateful and thank you, God for bringing us safely together and please continue to protect us and inspire us in your glory."

"Amen, Amen. I am so happy to be here Janice. I really, really need this." Annelle turned toward the bed where she put her suitcase and decided to unpack. "Hey Janice… What do you think is worse… being with an alcoholic or an adulterer?"

"What? What the hell are you talking about" Janice laughed. "How in the world do you go from gazing at the glory of God, to thinking about an alcoholic?"

"Well I just was wondering because we caught so much flack from so many people about the HBs and I mean… if a woman has been down the road and around the block of bad choices or circumstances, I just don't see how it's so wrong to have an HB!"

"It's not wrong. Well you know I don't think it's wrong. You didn't even know my Ronald was an HB which still cracks me up."

"I still can't believe you went behind my back and conspired with Walter to get Ronald. Geez, Janice. How could you…"

"Oh please, let's not go down that road again. I had no idea that you and Walter were falling apart the way it happened and I already had Ronald before Ted malfunctioned."

"Yeah. But you made me believe that you met Ronald at a party and that he was real…"

"Now even you would have been happily impressed if Ted hadn't fallen apart. The goal was to make them 'more real', remember? I mean after you were pregnant I was shocked that Walter approached me about Ronald, but it sounded like a good idea and we wanted to surprise you. He was so happy about the way Ted had worked his way into your life and he told me that you had given them a lot of information that led to some enhancements in Ronald, and it worked because even you didn't realize that he's an HB."

"Well… I'm glad for you… I guess. I am just feeling a little bit conflicted about it all now…"

"Which is why you got fired. I never thought Walter would do it, but I do understand that he had to because you were clearly traumatized by being so intricately involved in HBs and their development. I think Walter was right to let you go actually. You're still getting paid by them… forever."

"Yeah. And you're right. I agree it was time for me to step back. This vacation was the right idea at the right time and I plan to make the best of it."

"That's what I want to hear! Now as to your question… it's equally bad in different ways in my opinion because in both situations, both the alcoholic and the adulterer will drain your spirit with negative vibes and space all around you. But the physical effects can be totally different, yet equally dangerous in so many ways. I'd have to say that if those were my choices, I'd go for the HB."

"Well… I asked the question at a dinner I went to a couple of weeks ago and two of the women there said they'd rather have an alcoholic than an adulterer. That's incredible to me" Annelle said, shaking her head.

"It's not so incredible, unfortunately, Annelle. Some women have that martyr syndrome going on and feel like they can 'fix a man'... and usually to their own detriment. Me, I'd take the adulterer over the alcoholic if those were my only choices, but not knowingly..."

Then a knock on the door stopped their conversation and Janice went to answer it while Annelle continued to unpack. It was Candace who decided to come up and join them until they were ready to go to lunch.

"Stacey's on her way here from the airport, finally! She was complaining when she called me about a friend she had convinced to pick her up to bring her to the airport but she left so late, she ended up in bumper to bumper traffic. We'll be hearing this story all weekend" Candace laughed. Annelle and Janice laughed too because they know Stacey as well as her friend Candace does, whom they had just met.

Janice stopped laughing and got serious just to say "it's her own fault as usual and we're just going to have to shut her down if she tries to ruin our good mood with her attitude about missing the flight because we already know she ain't taking responsibility for it."

All three shook their heads in unison while talking about how predictable it was that Stacey would miss the flight, and marveled at how people who are habitually like that, make endless excuses and seem to never learn that they can remove that kind of chaos from their lives. However, Janice was emphatic about the effort to have a beautiful, uplifting vacation. They all agreed that they should make the conscious effort to choose serenity and feel the beauty of their surroundings. They took each other's hands before leaving the room and all agreed that they will consciously make the effort to be engulfed with every fiber of their being, by the love of God that they were so grateful for, and in appreciation of God's grace, they planned to honor it by regarding their temple of body, mind, and spirit as the gift that will be nurtured, pampered, and protected. They made a pact that their vacation would be the reinforcement to continue in that regard going forward in their lives.

They left the room and headed for the restaurant to meet the others and when they stepped off of the elevator, there was Stacey standing at the check in counter in the lobby. She had her back turned to them and appeared to be arguing with the hotel clerk.

"Look at her. Arms flailing around like a crazy person. Stacey! Why didn't you call me when you got here? I have your room key already. We're already checked in." Candace raced over to Stacey with the key card in her hand. Stacey turned with a grimace on her face and was clearly not ready to leave the counter.

"Oh! Well I was just trying to make sure that I receive points for the room…"

"But I told you that I received the points because I booked the room on my card…"

"I know… but I was trying to find out if I can pay half of the cost on my card so I can get some points too…"

Janice stomped her foot on the floor and said, "Oh damn Stacey! Please don't start off this way… let it go! Geez! We're headed to the restaurant to meet Patlyn and Sheila. Why don't you let Candace show you where your room is and then come on down to have lunch with us." Janice was determined to not allow Stacey to drag their aura down. Stacey stood there looking annoyed for a second and then after seeing the expression on Candace and Annelle's faces, agreed with Janice's suggestion. The hotel desk clerk looked relieved as Stacey grabbed her papers off the counter and turned to grab her bags since she didn't allow the bellman to help her. Candace grabbed one of Stacey's tote bags from her to help her along to the elevator when Annelle turned to say…

"Hi Stacey. So nice of you to join us for this wonderful occasion…"

Stacey stopped and turned and realized that she hadn't even uttered a greeting when they approached her at the hotel desk, she hadn't even said hello. Annelle and Janice walked over to Stacey and gave her a hug, and told her to relax, put her things upstairs and come on down to lunch so that they can chat, eat, and go over the agenda that Janice put together.

2 THE GETAWAY - AGENDA

When Annelle and Janice arrived at the restaurant, Patlyn and Sheila were already there, each having a Mimosa. Janice beamed a bright smile and said, "Welllllll….. Good afternoon ladies! I see y'all aren't waiting to get your groove on. Stacey just arrived so we're all here."

"Oh that's great. These Mimosas are sooo delicious and refreshing!"

They all laughed at Patlyn sounding like a commercial as she let out a satisfying AHHHHH after taking a sip. They sat down and Janice passed out the agenda she created, along with a couple of pamphlets and flyers she had collected to back up her choices with more details, as well as give them other options if they decide that didn't want to do the things that she had highlighted. Sheila had been pretty quiet up until she received the agenda and materials that Janice had passed out.

"Oh this place is so beautiful. I am so glad I'm here… I really need this. I am definitely joining you all for the Spa Treatment day… I can't wait…"

"Oh I've arranged for them to bring us a couple of bottles of complimentary wine and a fruit and cheese plate while we're there. But let's wait until Stacey and Candace get here to talk about it because I'll need to call the spa and let them know if we all intend to do this package, and let them know which specific treatments that each of us would like."

Janice was thrilled to hear Sheila's affirmation which gave her the opportunity to begin explaining more about it in her effort to motivate and encourage them. Janice urged them to review the materials and then remembered how hungry she was and decided to pick up her menu instead. The others followed suit and decided they should order a couple of appetizers while waiting for Stacey and Candace to come down. The waitress came over and they settled on ordering the Veggie Lettuce Wrap appetizer, Fried Calamari and Tortilla Chips with jalapeño-spinach dip. Patlyn saw Stacey and Candace enter the restaurant.

"Here they come… Over here y'all."

"Hi Patlyn."

"Stacey, this is my friend Sheila, she's from Detroit." Patlyn stood up to point out Sheila while letting them get past her to the two open seats.

Stacey looked over at Sheila and before even saying Hi, she said "Detroit? Oh wow. Do you still live there?"

"Yes" Sheila replied. "They finally determined that our area wasn't toxic so I decided to stay…"

"Oh that's not what I heard. Ain't no way I would have stayed there after all those folks that looked like lepers started showing up in those hospitals…"

Before Sheila could respond, Patlyn jumped in. "Well Stacey, they found out that those people had migrated from the east coast…"

"I don't believe that." Stacey cut her right off as she geared up for a debate, but Janice wasn't having any of it.

"Uh girls… can we sit down and eat? I'm starved!"

Janice interrupted that banter immediately because she didn't want the mood of the afternoon to turn sour, and those who knew Stacey, knew that she was still carrying her dark cloud around, looking for someone to take her frustration out on after arriving there late. Stacey and Candace took their seats and picked up the menus and before Stacey even read the first word she said…

"I don't eat meat so…"

"Stacey, we ordered three appetizers, none of which include any kind of meat, unless you consider Calamari as meat" Janice said as she shook her head and then she began to review the entrees and noticed that they had Bluefish on the menu.

"I thought Bluefish was an Atlantic Ocean fish? Isn't it illegal to sell seafood from the northern Atlantic? I'm wondering how they could have gotten Bluefish anyway because everything that was living in the north east coastal ocean was killed off."

"Maybe the Bluefish migrated up to Canada or further south. Either way, I'm not ordering it. I'm going to get something safe like a Buffalo burger."

"Ha! You think that's safe, Annelle? I heard that those Buffalo on those ranges in Montana were walking around with five and six legs…"

"Oh shut up Patlyn! I bet you think that Chicken is OK, but I heard that they're raising them underground with artificial sunlight on genetically enhanced corn feed".

"Enough y'all! Damn!" Janice folded her menu and put it on the table, laughing and shaking her head. "Y'all know how to ruin a meal. I'm going to ask the waitress about their menu so that we can put our fears to rest."

Once the waitress arrived with their appetizers, Janice asked about the

Bluefish, and the waitress told them that they get their fish from the Caribbean Sea, and that they're not exactly the same fish as people from the northeast were used to. She assured them that their chickens came from a farm in Mexico and were free range birds, not mass produced in those underground facilities. She also told them that their beef and pork came from Mexico and were raised with organic feed, which was imported from South America. They were all more at ease after hearing all that and went ahead and ordered their lunch, although no one took a chance on ordering the Bluefish or chicken. They settled on some of the South American tilapia dishes and the Buffalo Burger platters.

"Ummmm. I haven't had a burger in so long. I figured I'd have at least one burger during our vacation for nostalgic purpose, but I plan to eat light and healthy for most of the days while we're here."

"You usually eat healthy anyway, Annelle," Janice interjected. "…so one burger won't kill you. Let's enjoy our lunch and talk about our agenda."

"Count me out for the Horseback Ride tour. I'll find something else to do on that day" Stacey blurted out right away.

"Come on Stacey. It'll be fun! The tour lasts for only two hours and we will be taking a ride through some of the most beautiful landscape to a river canyon…"

"I don't think I'm going either, Janice. I have never been on a horse" Sheila said.

"OK so I'm not alone! We can find something else to do Sheila" Stacey said.

"No. Sheila is going on the Horseback Ride tour with the rest of us" Patlyn said as she turned to Sheila to remind her about what she had said before… "You said that you wanted to try some things that you've never done before. That's what you told me Sheila…"

"I know, I know. OK… I guess I'll go."

"Don't let her talk you into anything you don't want to do…" "Shut up Stacey!" Annelle and Janice both said in unison, and then they all laughed.

They finished their lunch and sat there for a while talking and laughing, and then lounged around for the rest of the evening.

The next morning, Annelle had gotten up earlier than the others and had gone to the fitness center to get her blood pumping, and get good and sweaty. She was able to close her eyes while working out on the elliptical machine and reflect on how lucky and blessed she truly felt. Working out in the gym or taking fitness walks always relaxed her mentally and physically and she always felt like her spirit was renewed when she got a good, vigorous, sweaty workout going. Once she left the gym, she went back to her room and took a shower and Janice was still asleep, but stirred to the movement Annelle was making in the room and asked her why the hell she was up so early as she turned over on her other side and went back to sleep. Annelle knew she wasn't expecting an answer and just kept on moving through her routine and as she stepped into her steamy shower, she allowed her muscles to absorb the warmth of the water and felt her shoulders release. She hadn't realized just how stiff her muscles were until she felt the abrupt release that made her think that rigor mortis must have set in while she was still standing and breathing, and the shower somehow innervated her muscles back to life. She let the warm, almost too hot water run across her neck, across her sore shoulders and upper back, down her back and then she turned to allow the steamy water to rain down onto her chest, feeling the release of her chest and arms and it was so relaxing that she let out an audible sigh. She turned once again to allow the water hit her shoulders and then reached behind her to turn the knob a 'smidgen' more to the hot side and her muscles seemed to melt. She wanted to stay there even longer, but the thought of coffee floated into her brain and that moved her forward into, washing her hair and lathering up with some luxurious, scented lavender shower gel. She finally got out of the shower, put some lavender, relaxing lotion on and then she put on some really comfortable clothes of warm desert colors. She was really feeling good and ready to start her day with a nice latte and a magazine.

Janice finally woke all the way up before Annelle left the room and told her that she'd meet her down in the café for breakfast. Annelle was fine with that because it would give her a chance for some solitude to have her latte and skim through her magazine and collect her thoughts. She stepped out of the room and went down to the café. There were only a few people milling around the lobby and she decided to order her latte and then take a seat in one of the more comfortable chairs right outside of the café near one of the huge windows that gave an exquisite view of the red rock mountains. The early morning sun cast such a soft light and the sky was actually looking more like a soft, light blue. As she sat there, she noticed that she was having one of those moments where everyone seemed to look familiar. Everyone looked like someone she knew or had seen before. It was weird. As she watched people pass by with familiar faces, she began to wonder what their occupations were. It was like a game to her. As one woman walked into the café, Annelle decided that she must be a Vice President of some insurance company. She decided that the woman's lines in her forehead came from the stress of dealing with long hours at work trying to prove she was worthy of competing with her male, executive counterparts. The thought caused Annelle to shake her head as she muttered "You'd think things would have changed more for women in the workplace by now".

Finally she snapped out of her gaze and diverted her attention from the people stirring around and decided to flip through her magazine. She turned a couple of pages and then she glanced over to the concierge desk and saw Stacy standing there, looking aggravated, as usual. *Oh lord,* she thought and actually hesitated from moving to let Stacey even know she was sitting there. She watched her talking to the man behind the desk and didn't say anything until she saw Stacey turn around and see her. Stacey waved, and then turned to talk to the concierge for a few more minutes and Annelle was slightly aggravated, because she knew that it was the end of her relaxing latte time. She didn't get a chance to refocus before Stacey walked up to her.

"Hey Annelle! You're up early… Oh wait. You're always up early… what am I thinking…"

"Yeah well I wanted to get a workout in this morning and you know I like the quiet time of morning to start my day."

"Oh yeah… you're still like that, eh? I wish you had let me know you were going to the fitness center because I would have tried to get up to go with you."

"Oh please, Stacey. Don't even try it… you know you are not getting up early like I do, to work out."

"Yes I will…"

"Well I'll let you know if I go again early, but you'll have to set your alarm because I'm not calling you."

"OK… I'll show you…. You'll see" and she walked over to drag a chair over to where Annelle was sitting. Annelle was all in her head annoyed, thinking that Stacey better set her alarm and make her way down to that fitness center on her own if she wants to work out because Annelle likes her solitude and meditative opportunity while she works out. Stacey sat down in the comfortably upholstered chair next to Annelle and let out an exasperated sigh, as she flopped back into the chair.

"All I wanted to know was if they provided transportation to the casinos in Laughlin. It's a three hour trip on the road, but I figured I'd go there while you all are riding those smelly horses."

"You know, it would be nice if you'd at least try to do something different while you're here. Janice put a lot into creating an agenda for healing, relaxing and encouragement for us."

"Yeah well, she didn't ask for any of our opinions now did she? She always thinks everyone wants to do what she chooses. Well I spent my money and I'm going to enjoy it my way."

"OK. I was only suggesting that you might find it beneficial to engage in our activities because she has managed to get a spiritual life coach to join us on the ride. You really should come."

"Why can't she have the life coach speak to us during breakfast or lunch? Why do we have to ride a horse to hear what this woman has to say?"

"Oh boy... never mind. Aren't you going to get some coffee or something? It's a beautiful morning and thank God, that the sky has cleared up to the point that it's almost blue again after all these years. It's going to be a beautiful ride where we will be experiencing magnificent views of those red rock monoliths that sculpt the environment. I am soooo looking forward to this."

"I'll bet you are after all you've been through. I'll be right back, I'm gonna get some coffee."

Annelle was annoyed that Stacey interrupted her and especially with her last comment, but she also felt pity towards her because she is still one of the most aggravated persons she has ever known, and she always wished that Stacey would somehow find a way to enjoy life. Being around Stacey usually made Annelle feel much more grateful for her own life, in spite of all the trauma she'd been through. Annelle peered into the café and watched Stacey complain about how much the coffee cost, and chuckled to herself as she shook her head.

Stacey came back, sat down and said "Damn. Can you believe how much they charge for coffee? The price was supposed to have come down after we became the North American Union. The coffee plantations in Mexico have been doing very well so I just don't get it."

"Well you know, everything is so questionable about our commerce and trade still, especially now that the government is trying to pass off so much of the cost of moving all government offices to Nebraska from Washington DC. I mean, they said in the beginning that with our new Amero currency, we'd regain a stronger position economically in the world after that nuclear event..."

"War is what you mean. Everyone knows that Iran tried to hit Israel with their nukes. They missed their mark, that's all and it ended up in that desert. I'm just surprised that it didn't go farther than it did."

"Me too. It was so scary back then and so many people suffered, and still are suffering all over the world. I really do believe it was a meteor that started it though."

"Oh, you're one of 'those' people who just can't face the truth. Russia and Germany officials are still not in full agreement that it was a meteor. They're still suspicious you know."

"Yeah, I know. But somehow I keep wondering if Russia used this meteor event to encourage the nukes that followed because it's kind of strange that they didn't bother to shoot of any of theirs, yet they are the ones who told the U.S. that Pakistan was planning to strike us. It's a good thing that the U.S. had those diversion missiles, although our coast was so badly affected in the end, anyway."

"Well the bomb that landed in India was dropped by Russia..."

"They said that it wasn't them, that it was the Pakistanis. I don't know.

I'm not sure that we'll ever know the real truth behind it all. It was just so crazy right after all that happened. And those radiation sickness clinics that sprang up were a real mess… turning so many people away claiming that they were OK, when they were really infected. What a mess."

"I know. But how about the screening of pregnant women and the forced abortions they carried out when they suspected some kind of deformity due to radiation exposure. That was real ugly."

"And that's how HBs became a viable option, although now, I feel we've gone too far."

Stacey rolled her eyes at Annelle and leaned back in her chair and took a sip before responding to say "I think it's terrible that we've resorted to robots for husbands. We need to be putting more effort into finding out why so many men are still turning up with sperm that isn't viable. And depending on where you live, women are having trouble producing viable eggs too."

"Well I'm not so sure about the reproductive feature and the effort to make HBs out to be 'real husbands' either now because there are so many intricacies that cannot be compensated for with the androids. I mean I do feel that the HBs are useful but I just don't feel that it's a good idea anymore to have women be so invested in the idea that it is a real man. I can usually tell an HB when I see one and…"

"Good morning ladies. Stop lying Annelle", Janice laughed. "You know you can't tell with the new ones girl, please!" Janice finally made her way down to the café and walked up on Annelle and Stacey's conversation. "You were shocked as hell when I told you that Ronald is an HB."

"Yeah but he's a new one" Annelle replied. "And, there aren't many of his models out in public yet."

Stacey asked, "How is Ronald, Janice? I still can't believe you decided to get one of those things…"

Annelle cut her off… "Be nice, Stacey. He's not a 'thing'… Here comes Sheila and Patlyn. Someone want to call Candace to see if she'd like to join us for breakfast? We should go have breakfast now since we have that Yoga session lined up for noon today. It's already 10:00 so we better get moving.

Annelle wanted to change the subject because she knew Janice would probably end up cussing Stacey out by the look on her face when Stacey called her Ronald a 'thing'. They all decided to eat in the restaurant that featured healthy vegetarian cuisine at the hotel. A burger entrée was included almost as an afterthought it seemed since it was way in the back of the menu, and in small print. Annelle quickly decided what she wanted.

"I think I'll have the whole grain waffles with veggie sausage patties. Ummmm! It sounds so good."

"I think I'll have that too, Annelle." Janice leaned back in her chair and saw Candace come in. "Oh hi Candace. Decided to sleep late, eh?"

"Not really. I was sitting out on the balcony of our room having coffee. It's just so beautiful out here. Hey Janice, is the spa treatment day tomorrow?"

"No we are doing the Horseback riding tour tomorrow so we'll have to be up early to get there. A shuttle will be coming to the hotel to pick us up."

"Great! I'm looking forward to it. Have you decided whether you're coming or not yet Stacey?"

"No... I haven't made up my mind yet. I think I'll have the tofu scramble with home fries soufflé. You ready to order Candace?"

"Yeah. I'll have that too. I was sitting on that balcony in the room and had to smile to myself..."

"That's really nice Candace. I'm so glad you're feeling the serenity..."

"No girl! I was feeling my fabulous date I had the day before I flew out here. Oouuuu that man is so fine. He just makes my toes curl..."

"Damn Candace, we don't want to hear this shit you ol' slut. I'm glad I didn't fly out here with your ass" Stacey laughed.

Candace laughed too, and went on to explain, realizing the others were waiting to hear more.

"Oh be quiet Stacey. He's there when I need him but I ain't got to own 'em."

Annelle laughed when Candace said that. "Wait, what, is he married?"

"Well... yeah. But I didn't know it when I met him."

Janice's mouth flopped open and Stacey was clearly disgusted by Candace's affair.

"Well he ain't never gonna be yours" Stacey exclaimed as she looked around for the waitress and catching her eye, waved to her to let her know they were ready to order. But Candace was unashamed and went on...

"And that's the good part! He's his wife's problem!"

They all laughed when she said that, except Stacey who just grimaced at Candace. She turned to Annelle and said "She'd be better off with an HB than fucking someone else's husband".

"Stacey!" Annelle yelled even though she didn't want to engage in the conversation. But Janice did, and said "I ain't trying to be judgmental, but I have to agree with Stacey on that point."

"Well I ain't looking for y'all's approval... I'll just leave it right there" and Candace sat back with an expression that let them know she didn't give a damn how they felt about it.

The food arrived at the table and they all dug in. While they were eating, Sheila who had been quiet the entire time since they arrived at the restaurant, rather abruptly, spoke.

"I love my HB William. But I wish I could get him upgraded with the new features they keep sending me information about."

All of them at the table stopped for a moment and looked at her, and Annelle dropped her fork.

Annelle finally found her voice after a moment of shocking silence. "You have an HB Sheila? The William model? Wow! How come you never said anything about it til now?"

"Well… I'm not really in the habit of telling folks because I've gotten so much flack when I first received him. I won him in a contest."

"What!" I just don't understand how y'all can have those robots in your lives like that", Stacey blurted out. "Patlyn, did you know? I have never heard of any contest like that. Wow!" Stacey could not believe her ears.

"She only told me a few weeks ago" Patlyn said. Annelle was intrigued that Sheila was one of the women who actually won an HB. She hadn't really agreed with the idea originally, but then after some discussion, saw the benefit of putting a couple of them out there with people who otherwise would not have an opportunity to purchase one. She was thinking that had she had her experience with Ted before that contest, she would have never bought in to the idea. However, it did prove to be useful to the development team to put them out there. Annelle went on to explain to them that they did put three of the William model HBs out in selected areas as a contest for marketing purposes as well as for research, and then turned her attention toward Sheila, who seemed as if she wanted to clam up again, but Annelle being so intrigued, could not stop herself from questioning her.

"Are you still sending the surveys in to Nibiodymics? They're supposed to provide you with upgrades as long as you continue doing that."

"Yeah… I have always sent them in. I never missed one but after the first upgrade, they started charging for them, at a reduced cost. I wasn't expecting that… and it's expensive... I can't afford it. I wrote a letter and complained but I didn't get any response."

Annelle said that she would look into seeing if she could reach some of her contacts at Nibiodymics who weren't afraid to talk to her, about getting the upgrades because some of the changes were very significant. William was the third stage of the sexualized models but he had some language issues and was known to stall every now and then and had to be reset sometimes. Sheila seemed to open up more as Annelle talked to her and it looked as if she was relieved with the hope of getting some upgrades for her William.

"Y'all are some strange folks. Sick really. I'd rather use my vibrator than have one of those robots in my house…"

"Girl you don't know what you're missing. You can keep your ol' vibrator because my HB knows how to do it girl!" Everyone but Stacey laughed when Janice said that.

"Shut up Janice" Annelle said as she laughed. And just then, this fine looking man stepped into the restaurant. They all stopped and looked at him, and then at each other, and then back at him and behind him and around him to see if he had a woman with him, which he did.

"Damn! I knew he probably had a woman fine as he is", Stacey lamented. "And he's a real man too!"

"How the hell you know he's real, Stacey" Annelle said.

"I know how to tell if a man is real. All you have to do is feed his ass some collard greens and onions", and Janice and Annelle fell out laughing before Stacey could even finish because they remembered what Stacey was talking about. When someone tried to tell Bruce, that he was an HB at a party once and in front of everyone, he let out the most strident, hard, fart known to man. It sounded like it had to hurt it made such a loud, forced, crackling noise. It caused the entire room to stand still as if they had turned to stone. And then they all fell out laughing so hard that some of them were rolling on the floor. Stacey, Annelle and Janice were in tears laughing before they could even explain to the others what they were laughing about.

"Now that's how you know it's a real man!" Stacey said, as they all continued to laugh.

They were talking and laughing so loud that other patrons were turning, some chuckling along with them, and some looking rather annoyed at what they perceived to be a disturbance. Janice decided to pull out her itinerary to go over the activities for the day. She had told them that her focus during their stay at the spa resort was going to be meditation, spirituality, yoga and good healthy living, and she hoped that they desired that too. Her enthusiasm was radiating from her as she described the activities and what she went through to create an agenda for them. Her energy was infectious as the others chimed in that they were looking forward to getting started with her agenda, but Stacey was skeptical.

"What kind of yoga is this… you know there are many different kinds of yoga."

"Yes I know, Stacey. The yoga instructors that are available are Hatha Yoga specialists. The one I chose said that she usually taught Hatha Yoga because most people were more geared toward getting some physical fitness out of it, although she urges people to engage in Raja Yoga for its techniques that enhance spirituality and meditational benefits. She said she kind of integrates both flavors of yoga in her sessions. So why not just come to the first session and if you don't like it, there are other things I have listed that you might want to do, or of course, you can just decide to do whatever…"

"Oh geez, Stacey. Stop being so difficult all the damn time and just try it" Annelle snapped.

"I'm gonna come, Annelle… I was just asking, that's all… Damn."

Annelle and Janice said that they planned to attend all of the Yoga and

Pilates sessions that Janice included during their time at the spa resort. They finished their breakfast which was really brunch, and all agreed to meet at the fitness center for their first yoga class. Janice, Annelle and Stacey were already dressed in appropriate clothing but the others had to go to their rooms to change into comfortable clothes that are appropriate for Yoga. Sheila hadn't said much more at lunch after the 'William' conversation and unbeknownst to them, was undecided about going to the yoga class, but as they left the restaurant, she decided not to create more drama after seeing how they reacted when Stacey questioned it. She figured that maybe Yoga would help her relax and decompress. She was seriously worried that she wouldn't be able to find a way to relax although she hadn't told any of them that. So she decided to go through the motions to at least find out if it was possible.

Annelle, Stacey and Janice stayed behind at the table since they had some time before heading to the Yoga class and looked over the itinerary some more. Annelle said that she wanted to go to one of the group sessions that was planned to begin fifteen minutes after the Yoga session ended. It was a group discussion that focused on ways to deal with stress, depression and anxiety. Janice thought it was a good idea.

"You know, I thought you might want to attend that session. I know you've been holding up pretty well with all you've been through. Any positive reinforcement that helps your mental wellbeing is a good thing. I know how much you wanted the baby and had your mind so set on a family…"

"Yeah and remember… You have money in the bank and you're a PhD, smart as hell and can find a job anywhere" Stacey chimed in as she flipped through the pages of one of the pamphlets. Annelle didn't answer her, but just roiled a bit and acted like she didn't even hear her because Stacey always made comments like that in a way that almost made Annelle feel like Stacey resented her. Annelle actually hated the way Stacey seemed to trivialize everyone's issues but her own. She reminded herself of the drama queen that Stacey is and started thinking about how selfish Stacey can be also, but then decided not to dwell on it right then, but promised herself she'd find an opportunity to speak to her about it later. She was really in a physical, spiritual space that caused her to feel somewhat unsettled after they all had breakfast together, so she was looking to get grounded and calm. Her mind wandered back to how her mother and father always felt that going to church was the answer to everything, but she had stopped attending church regularly ever since she went to college. She had been so tired of the ol' 'go to church' mantra because she didn't feel that she was getting anything out of it, although she believed in the power of God and prayer. Now that her parents were gone, she had Janice always trying to push her back into the church, and she had been putting it off for years, but lately had been thinking more and more about reacquainting herself with a church.

"You alright Annelle?" Janice noticed that Annelle was 'lost in space'…

"Yeah. I was just thinking about how my parents were always trying to get me back into the church, and I see that you have found one for us to visit on Sunday."

"Well you know this particular vacation wouldn't be complete for me without finding some way to replenish my spirit with the word. I figured that since our priority is to focus and renew our physical, mental, spiritual selves, it would do us good to get some praise in as part of the process. I'm going to go to that talk with you after the Yoga session, Annelle. I think it will be an interesting discussion and I have some stuff that has been weighing me down over the years that I'm working on finding relief about."

Annelle was glad to hear that Janice was willing to go with her. Stacy said nothing at this point because predictably, she was not in a place where she could admit to herself that she needed that kind of help and was not open to feeling that it would be beneficial to her. She looked for ways to make herself feel better by dipping into someone else's distress and then comparing it to her life, deciding that others are worse off than she, so she must be OK. And then predictably, Stacey came right out and asked Annelle what was still getting her so down. Annelle just looked at Stacey who kept issues in a shallow place and tried to decide if it was worth her energy to try and direct Stacey to a place of empathy, which is what always seemed to be missing with her.

After pondering for a moment, Annelle went on to explain to Stacey that she was burdened by the idea that she was somehow instrumental in contributing to the destruction of the family unit, which was already in pretty bad shape. She had regrets after the fact, promoting the HBs the way she did, which became so popular an effort by the company. It wasn't that she thought it was totally a bad idea that they were providing a 'man', a household assistant, which was where she wanted to bring the focus back to. But they somehow seemed to go too far, and the company lost their focus on the societal impact and became solely concerned with the bottom line of profit that could be made with HBs.

"As usual" Stacey retorted and just looked at Annelle and shook her head as she went on…

"I can't understand how you could even care as long as you're getting paid and still receiving your royalties and dividends. You can relax and write a book or something, and find yourself a real man to have a family with. Something was probably wrong with that baby, that's why your robot tried to kill it."

Janice's mouth fell open and Annelle glared at Stacey and felt a heat rise throughout her body. She was so angry about the fact that no one seemed to believe her when she explained how Ted tried to kill her and the baby. She was even more upset that she was having second thoughts about what Ted intended to do. It made her feel so conflicted after Walter and the counselor at Nibiodymics tried to convince her that Ted had detected something wrong with the baby, but inappropriately tried to do a test that was set up in his program that would transmit information in that regard. She really deep down in her heart, did not believe that, but went along with the explanation because she had to admit that there was a chance that it was possibly true.

"Oh no you didn't just go there" Annelle shouted. "Stacey I am so tired of your callous ass. You can't even find it in yourself to even understand what it means to have a feeling. How did you get so cold? If I didn't know any better, I'd think YOU are a damn robot..."

"Stop. Stop it. We are not going down this road and let's just stop this right now. We are not here to tear each other down; we're here to lift each other up." Janice was standing up by this time as she was almost in tears pleading with Annelle and mostly Stacey, looking directly at her as she continued... "We've all been through a lot over the years and we need each other, especially in this world where there is so much turmoil and confusion. Let's make the effort to think about each other with some compassion and caring, because we know we do truly care about each other. Maybe we don't express it the same way but we know we love each other, right?"

"Right" both Annelle and Stacey said in unison.

"I'm sorry Annelle. I didn't mean to bring that up like that. It's just that..."

"It's OK Stace." Annelle cut her off before she could go any further.

Janice then looked at her watch and let them know that the class would be starting in fifteen minutes so they got up to head to the Yoga class. Stacey decided to go to her room first and found Candace was still there just finishing changing her clothes. Candace asked Stacey if she wanted her to wait for her, but Stacey told her to go on ahead and she'd meet her down there. Stacey went into the bathroom and for some reason, looked in the mirror, and for what seemed like the first time in a very, very long time, she really looked at herself in the mirror, and didn't like what she was seeing, she never did. She stared in that mirror for a few moments and tears began to well up as she became unable for a moment, to keep up her tough exterior, and keep her emotions buried. She felt devastated for no particular reason, and even more so because she could not remember the last time she had really actually looked at herself in the mirror. It was something incredible for her to actually ponder about... that she hadn't looked at herself in the mirror for years, even when she got out of the shower. She would look in mirrors to get dressed, but never actually look 'at' herself. It was more like looking through herself, or past herself. It was amazing how she managed to see, but not see herself in the mirror. She wanted to resume back into the denial she was most comfortable with about herself. But she was having a real struggle shutting the twisted image of her reality out. She knew she needed to go to that group session after the yoga class, which is what was bothering her, and she began to blame the whole idea of the weekend and Janice's agenda for her acute despair she was experiencing in the mirror. She decided that she would not go, as the face in the mirror grew back into the hardened, stoic, vacant expression she was used to, because in her mind, going to that group session might somehow cause the others to think that she could possibly have problems. *'They' have problems*, is how she liked to think about things, or she'd conclude that her problems are not as bad as theirs. And then, her usual face began to appear to her again. As she continued to stare in the mirror, her mind began to wind down a path that she had never been down before. She began to mumble softly as tears streamed down her face…

"If I have to continue living like this… Well, I'm not even living. I'm like the living dead. I have done everything right, and still, I don't have a man in my life. I have not ever met a man who is worthy enough to be with me. So what I'm overweight. I'm not as fat as a lot of women who are married… If I could finally just get my bills paid off I'd lose this weight. I can't believe I didn't finish college but I had to get a job. My mother was so stupid to leave my father! And she could have helped me pay for college… I don't know why they always treat me like some kind of outcast. And now she's paying for her own education… just selfish! I need to go back… I'm just going through the motions and feel like I have no soul, just a body that is dying a slow tortured death… why prolong the inevitable…"

And with that thought she scared herself and as if she had just awakened from a bad dream, turned abruptly from the mirror, grabbed a face cloth and washed her face and immediately put all those scattered feelings away, buried them deep inside a place where she hoped they would stay. She put on her stoic face, which she mistakenly believed, made her look pleasant, and headed for the Yoga class.

3 THE GETAWAY - SESSIONS

"Welcome ladies! Please grab a mat and find a space on the floor. You can remove your shoes and socks if you'd like, I choose to do yoga in my bare feet. Come on in ladies..." the instructor went on, greeting the women as they came into the room.

"We will be experiencing some of the basic positions in today's session as I explain my understanding of the cyclical nature of Hindu belief that I love to adhere to. It gives me some comfort with the idea that with all the horrors in the world, diminished morality and selfishness, and greed that led to such global destruction, we can be led to a rebirth and refocus of what is important in life in its most primitive of ideas in regard to living in harmony."

She then began instructing them in some stretching exercises and told them to make sure that they focus on relaxing, breathing and to remember to have fun.

They laughed at each other as they tried to manipulate their bodies into the poses as directed. They started off slowly doing seated twists and standing forward bends, which caused Sheila to blurt out "I think I broke my back" and they all fell out laughing. The instructor laughed too as she kept telling them not to strain their muscles or push themselves farther than their bodies were willing to go comfortably. The instructor then moved on to some more difficult poses like back bends and inversions, which caused the room to fill with audible moaning and falling all over the place as they so diligently tried to follow along. And then finally, the instructor showed them how to do the downward dog, the child's pose and ended with the corpse pose.

"That's my favorite one!" Annelle yelled out and they all laughed again as the instructor tried to get them into quiet relaxation of Savasana.

"That was really fun" Stacey said as they were putting their socks and shoes on and gathering their things.

"See? I knew you'd like it" Janice said. Have you decided whether you're going to the Stress seminar with us?"

Stacey didn't answer Janice and just continued to tie her sneakers, so Janice and Annelle looked at each other, shrugging their shoulders and headed out the door to the seminar in the conference room down the hall. Surprisingly, once they found their seats, Stacey came in, and so did Sheila. While they were sitting there waiting for the instructor to come in, Stacey asked Annelle why she was so interested in creating 'fake men'.

"You know Stacey… Here's the thing… I kept noticing how far we have sunk as a society and was so tired of seeing young girls walking around with that empty look… no expression at all… dead eyes as if there is no brain activity going on in them… no self-esteem, starving for attention any way they could get it. And it seemed like this diminished character was infecting girls at younger ages as time went on. Boys were growing up with no respect for women at all and love seemed to just be some kind of fantasy of the past. That's when I realized how much trouble we were in and how defeated people seemed to be, even before the nuclear event. So many people feeling defeated is a recipe for disaster and I just felt that we really needed to do something drastic to begin recovery in our society. So many women had given up on getting married and having a family, I figured HBs would at least help as a relatively short term solution that would lead to repopulate our world, especially after we've experienced such devastation. We've lost so many men due to wars, disease, and jail. And now so many men and women are infertile due to radiation sickness. We needed a new start… something different that would jolt our motivation."

Stacey was shaking her head as Annelle was trying to explain and finally exclaimed, "Wow. I mean, I'm sorry but I just can't see resorting to something so unreal. It's against God…"

"If it was against God, why do we have the knowledge necessary to create these options then? Ultimately, we were created to survive. This is just one avenue toward our continued survival" Janice interjected.

"To procreate with machines? It's just sick… come on!"

"Stacey, you yourself have not had a man in years… one that you feel is good enough to be with you. You always said you wanted a child, and you don't even know if you can have one…"

"I plan to get that test and maybe I'll adopt or get a foster child. I ain't having no machine fuck me!"

"Oh real nice Stacey. I guess you're against artificial insemination too? What's the difference?"

"You know there's a difference Annelle! You are trying to replace real men with robots. It's just wrong…"

"Good afternoon ladies! Welcome to the Stress Relief Seminar. What a wonderful way to begin your spa vacation experience, by joining us for some real discussion and good information on how to relax and let go…"

They hadn't even noticed the instructor walk into the room they were so involved in their conversation and Janice was so heated that she got up and moved her seat away from Stacey and sat next to Sheila instead. Sheila had been sitting quiet throughout the entire conversation, and was glad that it was cut off by the seminar instructor interrupting them. The instructor began by asking each of them to introduce themselves to the group and give a brief summary of one thing they'd like to let go of while they are there on vacation that impedes their ability to fully relax. After sitting in silence for a few moments, Janice raised her hand. Neither Annelle nor Stacey was surprised that Janice raised her hand, knowing her so long and well, and knowing that she was so motivated and enthusiastic about their spiritual revival. Janice had introduced herself and mentioned briefly how grateful she was for her friends and especially Annelle whom she called her sister in Christ, and the reason that she ended up living in Hammond, Indiana. She turned and smiled at Annelle, Stacey and Sheila as she fondly spoke about how wonderful it was that they all came together for a well needed and deserved vacation. And then, she said that she needed to get something off her chest so that she could find a way to forgive herself. Annelle and Stacey both looked at each other in disbelief at that comment because Janice seemed so 'put together' and strong, always being the shoulder that they could cry on. It was stunning to them that she stood and revealed that she had been holding on to some burdensome issue, and Annelle began to even feel a little guilty for not ever noticing that Janice could be burdened by something, and she became teary-eyed while Janice was speaking.

"I question myself every now and then… about my reasons for having an HB in my life instead of trying to get involved in a relationship with a real man. It's not like I'm ashamed of it or anything like that, but I just want to try and resolve in my own head, what my true motives are for having him… my Ronald. I mean… I am so grateful for the option and I think that this invention, creation of this kind of option is extremely useful for many reasons. But in the back of my mind, I keep wondering if I have turned to Ronald because I had been raped by my ex-boyfriend…"

Annelle's and Stacey's mouths dropped open for what seemed like a full minute as Janice went on without looking at her friends' reactions, because she wanted to get it out without getting all emotional. She went on to say how she had met him not long after moving to Hammond and they got along fine in the beginning, but she had tried to ignore some red flags that actually ended up turning their relationship into something turbulent. She admitted that she had to examine her role in the dysfunction because she was the kind of person who liked to take control. Either way, it just didn't work out and they had broken up. She paused for a moment to look at her friends whom were all sitting there looking stunned.

"He came to my home one day about four months after we broke up, and I don't know why I let him in... we had argued over the phone a couple of times when he tried to convince me that we should try to get back together, but I wouldn't go for it. Anyway... I let him in, even though I knew he had a new girlfriend. I mean... he had stopped by once before, and had tried to talk me into having sex with him 'for old times' sake', but I never gave in. But that last time I let him in... he raped me..." Janice dropped her head as her voice seemed to trail off into silence for a moment as she appeared to try and catch her breath so that she could go on. There were a couple of gasps in the room from other women but Janice continued to focus on the instructor, and did not turn to look at her friends at all, as if she all of a sudden couldn't face them after admitting that. The instructor softly asked her to please continue.

"I didn't call the police because I felt like it was my fault."

"Janice! Why didn't you tell me?" Annelle couldn't help but blurt that out and she stood up to go hug Janice, but the instructor asked Annelle to "please sit down and let her finish".

"I thought about calling his girlfriend but decided against it. I told him if he ever came back to my house again, I would call the police though, and I felt like he realized how serious I was because he hasn't come back to my home again. He called and left messages, apologizing and whatnot... I have not answered any of his calls... and maybe a couple of months afterward, he stopped calling and I have not seen him or heard from him again. And here it is a couple of years later, and I have this HB... Ronald. And I love my Ronald. I feel safe with him..."

You could hear a pin drop in the room it was so silent. She looked around and then apologized for taking up so much time with her story. The instructor assured Janice that it was alright and said that she was so glad that Janice came, then asked for a show of hands if there were any others in the room who could identify in some way with her experience and there were a couple of hands that went up, including Sheila's.

"Before we go on, I'd like to say that the first step to getting past your issue is to forgive yourself. We will talk more about that once everyone introduces themselves" the instructor said as she began writing on the flip chart that she had on an easel that stood in the front of the room. She allowed the rest of the women to introduce themselves, and express any issues that they wanted to be relieved from but after Janice set the tone, the discussion seemed to lean toward the issue of forgiveness, relationships and the controversies surrounding HBs. Aside from Annelle, Janice and Sheila, there was one other woman there who had owned an HB, but had since returned him. That woman went on about how she loved the way he helped around her house, but she couldn't seem to get used to him beyond that. She also revealed that the pastor of the church she belonged to was so set against HBs that she began to feel guilty for having him. Hers was an earlier model that came after Brad, and that model was still very detectable by the general public, as being an android, or robot as many people referred to them.

When it was Sheila's turn to speak, she said that she was happy with William, her HB, and she only wished that she could get the enhancements that were prescribed by the company. With that, Stacey finally interjected that she thought having an HB was like a 'cop out' for women who didn't want to go through the trouble to make themselves acceptable to real men.

"Y'all have given up. And Annelle, you have invented a way for women to give up on real men. Women need to work on themselves to become more acceptable and willing to be wives"

"But look at you!" Janice interjected. "You haven't been in a relationship for years and always saying that you're working on you… That sounds like a 'cop out' to me. You believe you're inadequate for a man as you are now? Well that's your problem… and you need to work on that low self-esteem…"

"You shut up Janice! You think you're so damn perfect, yet you fell in love with a robot" Stacey yelled.

"Ladies! Ladies! Please! Let's all sit back and take a deep breath; breathe in…, and release. Let's do it again; in… and release. Good. Now, you all are good friends. We're not going to leave here with any animosity. It is mutual respect and understanding that we must remember. Can we all agree on that?"

They all nodded, but Stacey was so emotionally annoyed with the discussion her face remained grimaced and she couldn't let it go…

"I just want to know. What would drive a woman to decide to give up on humans? I mean, what happens in a woman's life that would make her decide that a robot is better. I understand the sex part… kind of. At least there's no chance of catching a disease from some stranger. But women are actually marrying and having babies by these robots. I just think its nauseating… Annelle, you haven't had any really turbulent relationships that I know about. What in the world at your young age, has caused you to decide that real men aren't good enough anymore.…"

"That's not it Stacey! You have to admit, men have become more scarcely available over the years as more and more women were deciding to have children on their own. Some women admit that as a reason they've even turned to other women, as lesbians because of the companionship that people crave with family and being in loving relationships. Come on… even you haven't managed to find a man…"

"That's because I'm still working on me and also, I don't just settle for any man… but I know that there are men out there that want to be in relationships that have jobs and want families. You just think you're too good for a real man. That's what I think…"

"What? How dare you say such a thing. That's not it at all…"

"OK, OK ladies. This is an issue that will not get resolved here today, but we can at least leave here with the goal in mind to accept each other's choices in life and respect each other. We all must be supportive, rather than judgmental and if we learn to have more empathy and compassion, Janice, for example might have felt more at ease with sharing what she had gone through with a good friend. We all need each other because 'no man, or I should say no woman, is an island'. Annelle mentioned feeling some guilt for not realizing that Janice had even had any deep issues that bothered her, and felt that it was selfish. Well we should all hold on to some degree of selfishness, in that we should take care of ourselves and our wellbeing so that we can be there for someone else. Let us all leave here today and promise out loud, to wake up each morning with a positive affirmation to set the intention of each day. I've provided you all with a list of affirmations and you can also make up your own. This has been a wonderful, powerful session, ladies and I have learned a lot myself as this world has changed so much over the years. Thank you for coming and if you have signed up for the meditation session on Thursday, I will see you there."

They all got up and filed out after choosing one of the positive affirmations to say out loud. Stacey said that she was going to her room to grab her book, and planned to go sit out in the garden with a tall Mojito, and relax. Although Annelle, Janice and Sheila said that sounded like a good idea, neither of them chose to join her, but all three decided to go for a walk down to the river canyon that was nearby before they all met for dinner.

"What time are y'all planning to be at the restaurant?" Stacey asked.

"Meet us there by around 6:00 PM. Can you make sure that Candace knows? It's on our agenda anyway" Janice replied as she continued to walk away with Annelle and Sheila.

"OK, if y'all run into any 'real' men, send them out to the garden where I'm at… OK?" Stacey laughed as she said that and Annelle yelled back to her "go to hell" jokingly, but she was really annoyed.

"She really gets on my nerves with her attitude about HBs. I'm glad she took her ass out to the garden. She's always so critical and unable to see things any other way than through her narrow eyes."

"Now Annelle, we're supposed to be in positive space right now, right after leaving that session…" Janice grabbed Annelle's arm and gave her a gentle shake to try and get Annelle to 'shake the anger off'.

"Oh yeah, that's right. Well that's another good reason for separating from Stacey right now then!"

Janice and Sheila both nodded in agreement and they continued to walk outside and toward the trail that led down to the river in the canyon. It was incredibly beautiful as the sun beamed down onto the sculpted mountains that it seemed to force serenity into their spirits and all three began to feel calmness seep throughout their bodies as they strolled down the path. Annelle began to recite some of the affirmations that they had received from the seminar and Janice joined in by stating how blessed they are to be able to enjoy such a place. She then turned to Sheila who had been silent since they left the seminar.

"Sheila, are you always this quiet? You barely had anything to say in the seminar..."

"I'm just taking everything in and really feel at peace. I am so glad I came, believe me. I am truly happy to be here, and especially to be here with the woman who invented HBs. No matter what Stacey says, there are a lot more women out her who thank you for your efforts."

"I appreciate you saying that."

Annelle didn't want to burst Sheila's bubble by venting about how conflicted she felt after Ted, to the point where she feels that the HBs may be a mistake, at least in the way they're currently being used. She decided to let it go for the time being, and allow herself to feel good for women who are happy with them. She actively pushed her conflicted feelings away by taking a deep breath and looking up at the almost light blue, slightly lavender sky. They reached the river and sat down on the edge of a rocky ridge and said nothing to each other, as each of them gazed into the beauty of their surroundings. After almost five minutes of silence, Janice looked at her watch.

"Well ladies, we should head back so we can meet the others for dinner."

"Yeah, my stomach is growling. I'm famished" Annelle said. "You ready Sheila?"

But Sheila seemed to be in a trance, and hadn't moved, nor acknowledged that Janice and Annelle had gotten up. Annelle and Janice had only met Sheila on this vacation so they figured that maybe she was the quiet, contemplative type of person.

"Yo girlfriend! You coming?"

Annelle's play-acting voice like some old 'hip-hop' language jolted Sheila out of her trance and she seemed startled for a second, but then smiled and jumped up from where she was seated and skipped toward them as if she had some renewed energy.

"Yep! I'm ready to eat. Ugh! I was thinking about some of the things I need to do when I get home and..."

"Oh no... we're not supposed to be thinking about work and what needs to be done at home while we're here… remember?

"I know Janice. I couldn't help it, but I am gonna try to let go while I'm here. Let's go, I'm starving too."

They all met up at the restaurant after the various activities they participated in and filled each other in on their experiences so far. Sheila sat quiet as she listened to Janice and Annelle talk about finding relief from some of the baggage they carried around, and she longed to be able to relieve some of her own, but knew she would drag her baggage around with her for the rest of her life. She vowed to herself that she would keep her secret between 'herself, God, and the gatepost' as her grandmother used to say. It had been over ten years since George had died and no one knew how glad she was that he was gone, forever. Her mind wandered around her reasoning that she had to rid herself from him for good, as she did every now and then and always managed to convince herself that there was no other way. As far as she could tell, no one really cared much that he died, but only acknowledged that he was gone. The seminar caused her to yearn to relieve herself from the tremendous burden she carried regarding what happened to George, but her subconscious took over every time and worked to keep her mouth shut and bury it deep down inside and hold it in.

"Earth to Sheila" yelled Patlyn.

They all laughed as she seemed to lurch out of her trance.

"What you thinking 'bout girl? You were all out in space somewhere…"

"Nothing…."

"Yes you were!" Patlyn barked. "You were thinking about that husband of yours. I don't know why you keep trying to act like his dying had no effect on you."

"It did! I found peace" Sheila almost shouted.

They all gave her a look of puzzlement once she said that, because peaceful was not the word any of them would have come up with to describe her. They had heard some of her story through the grapevine by way of Patlyn. Being that they were in an environment where the sole purpose and aura was to promote serenity, Patlyn figured that Sheila was in the right place, and could possibly arrive at peace, or at least learn how to make the effort to get there. They all agreed that she would get something out of being there, and ironically, Sheila's presence gave off some kind of tension that reinforced the others in their own efforts to fully engage in experiences at the spa resort once they heard Sheila say what she said…

"I found peace, and I am happy. I have William and I am very happy. Even my children are happy for me."

Sheila forced a smile onto her face and tried to look relaxed, and with that, they all picked up their menus and talked about what they wanted to order. Sheila had her menu in her hands, but she was finding it hard to focus as her mind wandered. She began to reflect on the way she stumbled upon that raffle ticket to win an HB when they first began resembling 'real men in real ways' as physical/sexual surrogates and companions. She was tired of being alone, but not desperate enough to ever end up with the type of man she had been with for too many years. She vowed to never again succumb to the type of shiftless, dependent of a man who had no clue what it meant to be responsible and accountable in life. So she took a chance when she happened upon that raffle ticket at the gym she worked at, and won.

George had died over ten years ago back in 2010. She had left him numerous times, but he would never accept it and like a bad cold, kept chronically returning, as she kept justifying reasons for letting him back in. Their children had seen a lot of dysfunction in their home that had unfortunately continued to play out in their lives the entire time they were together, and Sheila carried some guilt about that too. But once George was gone, it seemed like the air cleared around her and the palpable tension in their home was gone. Their son was two years younger than the youngest daughter she and George had together, and he was struggling in school and getting into a lot of fights. She had two other daughters who were older than she and George's daughter. Had it not been for the life insurance she had on George, she wouldn't have been able to get off of public assistance and she felt that posthumously, he was finally taking care of his family. She and their four children had moved on in their lives as if they could not wait to get away from the madness they had been living in.

"Hey Sheila, what you having?" Patlyn was determined to get Sheila out of her shell and decided that she should actively pay attention to make sure Sheila engaged in having a good time with them.

"Oh... I think I'm going to have the orange glazed salmon."

"Good choice", the waitress replied as she continued around the table to take everyone else's order. After the others gave the waitress their orders, Candace and Patlyn began to talk about their day and how they had taken the shuttle into a little town where there were art galleries and little boutiques. They recommended that the others be sure to include that activity in their plans before leaving to go home. Their voices began to drone on as Sheila began to zone out, unable to stop the trickle of memories she tried to keep from bubbling up to the surface. It seemed like the place they were at with all of its quiet and relaxing atmosphere, had removed all of the chaotic noise she had been so accustomed to at home, and allowed sensory receptors that were dull and buried, to come alive. She was experiencing feelings in the quiet calm of her surroundings that caused her to head to hurt, as she tried to push them back, bury her emotions and try to continue to forget. Annelle noticed that Sheila had drifted away and figured it was her turn to try and get Sheila to engage in their conversation.

"You know, it's really hard to actually let go when you're in a place where you're supposed to let go, because you're so used to being busy, moving from one thing to the next, managing activities, putting out fires with your kids, dealing with bills. We're going to have to help Sheila to relieve herself so that she can truly be here with us on this vacation, because it seems like your body is here, Sheila… but your mind is still at home, or somewhere…"

"I'm sorry y'all. You're right Annelle. I've been through a lot. I guess we all have, in our own way. Don't worry… I am enjoying this place. I'm looking forward to our Horseback riding trip too. That canyon is so beautiful."

Annelle was wondering all along, if Sheila was having issues with her HB, William. She didn't want to bring it up at dinner with Stacey around, but planned to get a chance to talk to Sheila in private, to see if she was experiencing anything 'odd' or even dangerous like she did. She also pondered about trying to figure out how to get those enhancements for Sheila because she felt that it was wrong for them to do the contest, but leave it to the winners to pay for enhancements outside of the lifetime maintenance warranty. But Annelle was way off in her assessment of what was bothering Sheila. Even Patlyn had no clue what was really on Sheila's mind. Their food came and they all ate heartily, had a couple of glasses of wine and even had dessert.

"I'm so full" Stacey said. "I think I'm going to go sit in the lounge and have a martini. Anyone game?"

"I'm in" Janice replied.

"Me too! I hear an apple martini calling me!" Annelle jokingly said.

"Come on with us Sheila" Candace said as she stood up from the table. "I know you don't drink… order a soda or something. They've got a live band that will be playing some country music in there… maybe we can kick up our heels with a 'do-si-do'…"

They all fell out laughing at Candace as she started kicking up her heels to demonstrate her rendition of that dance. But Sheila begged off and said that she was tired and planned to go sit in the garden to read before going to bed. Patlyn said that she'd go with her, but Sheila told Patlyn that she just wanted to be alone to get some reading done and promised her that she was OK, so they all went to the lounge without Sheila.

4 THE GETAWAY - SECRETS

Sheila went to her room to get her book and then down to the garden as she had said she would, because she knew that Patlyn or one of the others would eventually come looking for her anyway. She was feeling tense, and decided that she needed some kind of calming tea, maybe chamomile or something once she got down there. She grabbed her anti-anxiety pills and took two of them and was feeling really glad that she hadn't left them behind. She had actually considered leaving them home, believing that she wouldn't need them in such a nice and relaxing place since she was trying to stop taking them. But now was not the time. She thought about the sleeping pills she brought with her, but she knew better than to take them too early and decided to wait, as she repeated to herself that she had to figure out how to pretend that she is having a good time. And to do that, she had to put the madness of her past that was bursting forth, out of her mind. She was becoming angry as she sat down in the comfortable lounge chair out in the garden and felt that George was somehow punishing her from the grave, inhibiting her from relaxing and having a good time. However, thinking further made her feel glad he is gone out of her life, and she decided that she will not allow thoughts about him to mess up her vacation. Her defense kicked in allowing her to revisit her need to reinforce justification for what had happened.

Over the years before he died, George had managed to somehow acquire permanent disability. Sheila felt like he had finally wore out the people at Social Security and they just finally gave in, knowing that at his age, it was hopeless to even think he'd manage to make a living with all the complaints he continued on with about his back, which he always claimed kept him from getting a job. If he managed to get a job, he claimed that his back kept him from going to work every day. He'd find work on occasion, work for a while, and then find some reason that he couldn't go, or he'd be

38

insubordinate, or something. And since he had won a lawsuit after one of his many mishaps and accidents, he finally had grounds to make a case that he was disabled. His disability was more mental, than physical as he struggled through life with the kind of character where he could somehow convince people that he could do things that he actually wasn't good at. And then his inability to ever accept responsibility kept him from learning from his mistakes, always blaming someone or something else instead of ever having the courage to look within himself. Sheila's enabling nature didn't help him either, and over the years, George had deteriorated. He was self-destructive more and more by way of his weakness and it was her weakness that allowed him to be destructive to their entire family. Once his mother died, George felt such a sense of loss and it became yet another excuse for why he could not get himself together. It was peculiar since he didn't really see or talk to his mother much over the years. Still, his mother had become somewhat of a fantasy anchor for him after she died, and he missed her earthly presence once she was gone. This was piled on as yet another reason he used for not being able to function as a viable adult, and people who didn't know him were always left thinking that this poor man was so close to his mother and suffering her loss.

Sheila had sunk deeper and deeper into depression over the years that she was with George, and it was a friend who finally stepped in and forced her to get help. She was seeing a psychiatrist who prescribed antidepressants for her and also anti-anxiety medication due to her irritability and panic attacks. She was told by her therapist that she would have to become strong enough to resist being the martyr she had become over the years, and make a decision to be the breadwinner since she continued to allow George back after she would put him out, or commit to the decision to let George go to fend for himself, as he was one source of her stress and depression. However, she never found the strength to turn him away from her door when he would come back crying and begging to be let in. Sheila felt for years that she had no more fight left in her and had given up, but the therapy somehow managed to drill through the granite of her skull and some light 'eeked' in… She began to have hope for a brighter future. However, that hope involved some antifreeze, oatmeal, soup and chili.

Sheila came home from work one day and she had acquired the mental mechanism that allowed her to regard George as part of the furniture in the house. This became her reaction to him being there, in order for her to have the burden that weighed her forehead down just from the sight of him, lifted. It allowed her to disregard him as if he were background in their home, and sometimes when he spoke she wouldn't even react, it was like background noise the way the TV would be on with no one looking at it.

One day in particular, George had decided to surprise Sheila and their son by cooking dinner, which was unusual because she usually found him sitting in the recliner in front of the TV every night when she got home from work. He would sit there and wait until she got there and give her about twenty minutes before he would routinely say, "so what we eatin' for dinner?"

On that particular night, George had saved a couple of dollars from his allowance that she would give him from his disability checks. This was the newest condition at the time, that he offered for her to let him back into her home. He took his money and instead of buying a pint of cheap wine to share with his bum friends in the park, he went to the neighborhood grocery and bought three cans of Vienna Sausages and a large can of Pork and Beans. He was planning on asking Sheila for a couple more dollars so he could hang out with some of the guys from the neighborhood at the pool hall, and figured that making dinner would soften her up so that she'd pass off a few extra dollars beyond his allowance. He had planned to tell her that he was meeting a guy he had run into that morning while out buying the newspaper and he wanted to talk to him about a job, which was partly true, except that the old friend had already told George that he would let him work with him for a few dollars painting some rooms at a community center, if he was able to get the job. Sheila got home that evening and walked into the kitchen and was shocked to see George standing at the stove stirring a pot of something she could not identify by the smell. She stood there stunned for a moment, as if one of the living room end tables had suddenly come to life and found itself in the kitchen cooking something. And then she found her voice…

"What you cookin' George?"

"I had a taste for some 'vi-eenie sawcheses' and beans. Ain't had 'em in a long time. So I figured I'd cook us some dinner."

Sheila just stood for a minute, and then turned to go put her things down in her room and take her shoes off. She noticed the pillow on their bed that George had been sleeping on, stained with his saliva that he had drooled onto the pillow because he slept with his mouth open a lot, filling the room with the smell of his stale breath. Disgusted, she walked over to snatch the funky pillow off the bed and saw dead gnats stuck in the stain of the drool he had left there. She let out an exasperated sigh, and carried the pillow with the case on it, out of the room and dropped it near the door so that she could remember to toss it in the garbage the next time she went out. She went back into the kitchen and as she stood there watching him in his dingy tee-shirt that was too small to cover his stomach that hung beneath it, and felt a wave of what seemed like cement, pour into her forehead. The heaviness came on so strong she had no choice but to put her head down. She walked over to the kitchen table and sat down, propped her elbow up on the table and put her forehead in her hand.

George pulled three bowls down from the cabinet and grabbed the loaf of bread and sat them on the table. Sheila never looked up. As she listened to him scooping the Vienna Sausage/Bean mixture from the pot into the bowls, she began to feel psychotic. She started thinking of ways to get rid of him... permanently and for good. She reflected on a day she had taken off from work because of a migraine headache, an old re-run of The Montel Williams show about women whose husbands had left them and they had mistakenly killed their children using Antifreeze in their food, with the intention of making them sick so that their husbands would come back to them. She scared herself when she saw that show because she immediately began to plot in her head how she might pull such a thing off, ridding herself of George for good. But she never took that thought seriously, never believing that she could ever do such a thing, until that evening when he decided to cook dinner.

She saw the bowl appear in front of her held by his gnarled fingers and brittle, dingy fingernails. And her mind continued to spin the idea as she mechanically reached for the fork he placed in the bowl. She started eating, and he had told her to wait for their son and surprisingly, wanted to say grace...

"Lawd, please bless this here food I cooked and please bless my wife because she works hard and please bless my son and help him do good in school. Amen."

They began to eat and Sheila didn't even taste the food she was eating and never looked up. Meanwhile, George and their son 'chowed down' dipping the white bread into the sauce of the mixture to make sure they didn't miss one drop.

"Want some more Sheila? I cooked enough for us to have seconds."

"No thank you. I'm done and I have a headache. I'm going to lie down so make sure you don't turn that TV up loud".

"Oh. OK, well I was actually thinkin' 'bout going out... need a couple dollars though..."

"How much is a couple of dollars" she snapped, still, without looking up at him, although her face clearly grimaced as she spoke.

"Oh about ten I guess... I ran into Nooks at the store this mornin'. He been in town and I ain't even know it. He said he might have some work for me... so I figured I'd meet him tonight down at Smits Pool Hall."

Sheila got up, went into her room to get a ten dollar bill, went back into the kitchen and handed it to George. She told him to go on and she would clean up the dinner dishes. She wanted him to leave as soon as possible so that she could get to the store and pick up some Antifreeze. She was all the way there, in her head by now, contemplating and calculating how she will work it out, because she felt it was what had to be done. She believed she was putting him out of his misery, rather than recognizing how weak she had become in her own miserable life. She finished washing the dishes and cleaning the stove off after the mess he had made, splashing pork and bean sauce all over the place, and even that reinforced her idea that he had to go. Her nerves were raw and every little thing associated with him made her crazy, like she was going to explode and tear her own hair out. She heard George go out the door and her son had gone back into his room to do his homework. She leaned into her son's bedroom door to let him know that she'd be back because she had to go to the grocery store. She was moving with some sense of renewed energy. She no longer had a headache as her mind was occupied by the wheels that were turning as she began to think out the steps of her plan. She considered writing it down, but quickly discarded that idea because she knew she couldn't have hard evidence ever be channeled into reality, to ever be found.

She strolled down the aisles in the store, picking up various items, tossing a package of cut up chicken that was on sale into her cart, and then wandered down the canned goods aisle to toss in a couple of cans of green beans. She made her way down to the aisle where common household products were and slowly proceeded, scanning the aisle thinking that she'd find the antifreeze there, and then realized that it wouldn't be in that aisle. So she picked up a generic bottle of all-purpose cleaner and continued into the next aisle where there were automotive products. She couldn't even remember the last time she had gone into this aisle and she slowly strolled down, scanning both sides of the shelves and then saw it. Antifreeze. She picked it up and then immediately looked around and then tried to act nonchalant as she sat it down into her grocery cart. Then she almost froze as she thought about the time of year it was. It was September... seemed kind of early to be buying it she thought. She continued slowly down the aisle as she tried to come up with some kind of justification for buying Antifreeze in September. She then thought that it probably wasn't odd since they live in Detroit and proceeded through the self-checkout aisle to make her purchase.

Once she got home, she quickly took the Antifreeze out of the bag and placed it into the utility closet where they stored all kinds of cleaning items. She kind of hid it behind a huge container of laundry detergent, although it wasn't hidden. But she tried to sit it out of the way, and make it look as if it had always been there. It was still early so she didn't expect George back anytime soon, but when she turned from the closet, she was surprised by their son who had gone out while she was at the store and had come in while she was in the utility closet. He walked on past her and seemed to notice nothing out of the ordinary. She forced herself to act natural, and asked him where he had been, to which he replied that he had stepped out to see if one of his friends was around because he wanted to play with his friend's Xbox. He went back into his room, and Sheila continued to put the things away that she had bought from the store. She was thinking about how and when she would actually do it.

Over the next few weeks, Sheila helped George deteriorate with a daily dose of Antifreeze in his cereal for breakfast, or if she couldn't encourage him to eat oatmeal on a particular day, she'd make pudding dessert and put it in there for him, but she stopped using pudding though because one day her daughter stopped by and she caught her about to eat the poisoned pudding after she stepped out the room.

"What are you doing!" Sheila shouted at her daughter.

"I'm just tasting his pudding, he won't notice."

"No…. don't eat his pudding… I put some laxative in there because he hasn't been feeling well lately."

"Oh! Damn! I'm glad you stopped me.

That was such a close and unnerving call that Sheila almost abandoned the idea of getting rid of George that way, but as it turned out, he had already ingested enough to make him very ill. She had put some in his soup one evening and he actually commented on how good the soup was and asked her what kind of soup it was because it had an odd flavor. She had remembered reading that the sweet smell of ethylene glycol is probably what he was experiencing.

"Oh I added some seasonings to it just to flavor it up for a change"

"Oh. It taste real good. Ain't you having any?"

"I ate some already… that's why I poured all that was left into your bowl."

"I think I need to see a doctor. I been feeling ill lately… don't know what's wrong with me."

He ate half of the soup but couldn't finish it. By now, he had been ingesting antifreeze for a week, and began to appear drunk. Their son even asked him if he had been drinking, but George had replied no, he was just feeling sick. Sheila heard him say that and felt light headed for a moment as she realized that the poison was taking effect on him. That evening with the soup, George got up from the table and stumbled forward into the wall.

"George! Are you OK?"

"No. I think I'm sick. I must have a stomach virus…"

And then he threw up all over the floor as he tried to go for the kitchen garbage can. He grabbed the wall and Sheila ran over to him and sat him down in the chair in the kitchen.

"Oh my God, George! You must have the flu or something. Let me get you some Nyquil and you go and lay down. If you don't feel better by morning, then I'll take you to the doctor."

She was nervous about that part… and she decided to go to the library to read up on how the poison takes effect, so that she can be sure to not give any clue to the doctor. By the time she returned home, George had fallen out of the bed and had vomited up blood, which left a huge stain in the carpet. As he lay there, she stood looking at him without moving. Then she turned and went into the kitchen and made herself a cup of coffee, wondering if he was dead. She poured the coffee and sat down and drank it, then went back to the room and he was still lying there. She figured that he probably convulsed and choked on his own vomit, or maybe his kidneys had stopped functioning as she had read that is one of the effects from the poison. She stood there looking at him and then realized that her son could come in at any time, because he was down the street at his friend's house playing games on his friend's Xbox. She was amazed at how she had no sorrow for him as he lay there in a pool of vomit and blood. And then she realized that she had to call 911, but she wanted to make sure he was dead first. She reached down and poked his shoulder and he didn't move. Then she leaned over and looked at his face and his eyes were slightly opened, with such a lifeless look, that it startled her. She knew at that point that he was in fact, dead. She stood straight up and stepped backward toward the door of their bedroom as she focused on his back that wasn't moving. For a moment as she stared at him, she thought she saw his back move, like he might be breathing.

Sheila didn't panic, but began to go through the steps she had laid out in her head, to get rid of the antifreeze in her closet and take the garbage to a nearby dumpster, just to be safe. She put the antifreeze bottle into the trash bag that had his soup vomit in it with all the towels she used to clean it up, and then put it in her car and drove to a nearby development where one of her friends lived, threw it in the dumpster there, and then called her friend from her cell phone while she sat in the parking lot.

"Hey Sheila! How you doing?"

"I'm fine. I was just riding by and thought about you. I have the new Avon books you been asking me for. I was gonna drop them by since I'm in the area…"

"Oh OK. Yeah, come on up."

Sheila parked and went in as she had already planned this part too, so that when she got back home, maybe her son would find George on the floor and call 911. If that didn't happen, she'd call herself once she got back home, as she figured enough time would have gone by where he certainly could not be revived. She sat down for about ten minutes talking and laughing with her friend as if she found a new lease on life. She couldn't believe how she felt at that point. She looked at her watch and told her friend she had to leave because George wasn't feeling well and she thought she might have to take him to the hospital.

"Oh. He been drinking again?"

"Yeah well, that never stopped anyway, but lately he's been really ill. I kept telling him to go to the doctor, but he wouldn't go."

"Just like a man. Well, I hope he's alright. Thanks for bringing these books by. I'll call you later with my order".

Sheila left and drove home, the long way. She finally arrived and saw nothing happening, which meant that her son had not come home to find George lying on the floor. She had a chilling thought at that moment, like maybe George got up and left for the hospital. With that, she raced into the house and into their bedroom, to see him still lying right where she had left him. Finally, she reached for the phone and called 911.

The Emergency Medical Technicians arrived along with the police and Sheila went into her act, where she cried tears and explained how she got home and found him there on the floor. The policeman and one of the EMT persons went with her into the kitchen where she showed them the medication he was on for high blood pressure. They just nodded without emotion and then one of the EMT persons determined that he had already deceased, and made a call to the coroner. They questioned her without any sense of suspicion and quite methodically, made their reports and left, telling her that the coroner would be there shortly to pick him up.

Sheila was exhausted, more exhausted than she had ever felt before, and yet she felt wound up at the same time. She couldn't sit still and she paced from the living room, into the kitchen, back to the bedroom to see George lying on their bed where the EMT had left him. And then she thought about how she should probably call his cousin and let her know that George had passed away. She made a few phone calls to let people know he had died and one of her friends came by to assist her with mapping out steps she needed to take going forward with his funeral. Everything seemed to fall in place so naturally, and Sheila was able to mentally fall in step as if his death had been natural. The following week, she had him cremated after a small ceremony and that was the end of it, the end of a sad era in her life, yet it was not completely the end because she had begun to experience panic attacks and suffered terribly with debilitating anxiety that would keep her awake for many nights. Therapy did help her, although she never divulged to anyone what she had done to get rid of George. She had actually convinced herself over the years that he had died of natural causes and whenever the thought came up. That was where her mind went automatically. However, burying the truth was eating her up inside and wreaking havoc on her, physically.

A few years later, like some crazy and bizarre twist of fate, Sheila won the HB contest, and it couldn't have happened at a better time, when her friends and family were encouraging her to go out and meet people, go on dates and try to find a new man. She felt like it was God's message of forgiveness for her actions, which she reconciled in her own mind as necessary. And she did begin to feel better once she received William. She really felt that what she did was right and winning William proved it. She fell in love with William, even though her son hated that 'thing' as he referred to it, in her home. Her son had moved out and entered the armed forces, which was mandatory for two years once teenagers graduated from high school, and he felt some guilt about her getting so attached to William, because he couldn't be there. Her other children had moved on even before George had died and being that they are girls, seemed to understand more than her son, how and why she had become so attached to William. But it was people at Sheila's church who were making her crazy with their ignorant and mean comments. Even the pastor was against women having HBs in their homes, so Sheila left that church and had begun to visit other churches in her area on occasion.

And all these years later, she sat back at the spa resort with her book in her lap, and felt better once she reflected on how she arrived there, how William had helped her so much mentally and physically, how God had protected her through it all. That is what she told herself, it's what she wanted to believe, and she finally seemed to feel some calm, enough calm for her to open her book and read.

Just as she was getting deep into her book without being distracted by her thoughts, Annelle walked up and sat down in the lounge chair next to Sheila's.

"How's it going? Isn't it beautiful out here tonight? I decided to get away from all the noise and come out here and experience the beautiful night… Oh! I hope I'm not bothering you…"

"No, it's OK. I don't know how much longer I'd be able to focus on this book anyway. I was thinking about going on up to my room to go to bed. Our day starts early tomorrow anyway…"

"Yes, that's true. You know, I wanted to ask you about William. Do you mind talking about him?"

"Not at all" Sheila said as she placed her bookmark inside her book to set it aside. "I was hoping that we'd get a chance to chat, without…"

"Without Stacey around… I know. She can be a real pain in the ass. Just ignore her" Annelle said as she reclined in the lounge chair next to Sheila.

"Well, it's hard to ignore it all the time. I get flack from people in my neighborhood too. I had to leave my church because of William."

"Wow. Are you kidding me? You know… I gotta tell you, I keep being surprised at some people's reaction to the idea of why HBs were developed, but over the years, I've begun to understand some of the issues that cause people to be against it. Yet still, their issues don't address the root causes for why women would be so attracted to the idea of having an HB."

"I totally agree, Annelle. I mean, I was alone after my husband died for a few years… I had gone on a couple of dates. But I just wasn't about to take on another man who had employment issues, who drank or used drugs, or was violent…"

"I know. And it's not like all men are like that, but there aren't a lot of men around who are available, and I myself, am not into getting involved with any of those kinds of men you mentioned, nor am I going to involve myself with anyone's husband either."

"For real. It's not like I am against having a real man, Annelle. I just hadn't found one and maybe I carry too much baggage for a real man too. So whatever it was, I just thought it was a blessing that I won William. He has been so much help in my house too."

"Yeah… that is what most women like about their HB. It's a hard argument for men to make, because they aren't willing to cook and clean around the house like an HB will."

They both laughed when Annelle said that. They went on with their conversation and Annelle was careful not to express too much, how she truly felt about HBs since her incident with Ted, because she was still so conflicted about what happened, and also about the benefits of having HB versus not having them available. She was real interested in getting information from Sheila so that she could use it in the proposal she was working on, that she planned to approach Walter with. It kind of left a bad taste in her mouth that she would approach Walter, but she couldn't figure out a better way of getting her idea back into HB development since he was part owner of the patent, a decision she grew to regret.

"How did you come up with the name for these… androids?"

"HB? Home Boy? Oh. Well… when I was doing my thesis, I struggled on what to call them but I kept going back to my idea that it would be a home assistant for women, since there were so many women who lived without men. So many women who had children had to work. So I started thinking of it as a 'man in the home' to take care of the household. Then for some reason, 'pool boy' popped in my head, and I was thinking about gardeners that women hire and whatnot. And finally, I arrived at 'Home Boy'. I thought it was kind of catchy because it was a term used by a lot of people anyway when referring to their 'homies'… but Home Boy just seemed to fit. It wasn't long before the acronym became the more pronounced icon that stuck… HB. The fact that they can cook, do grocery shopping…"

"And that's what my William can't do. He can't do my grocery shopping, because he was the model that came out before they were approved for driving privileges. I wish I could get that upgrade because it would be a big help. I also heard that there are some language enhancements and I wish William could get that because he still sounds a little too automated. Most people don't know right off, that he's an HB, but if they're around him long enough, somehow they figure it out."

"If you don't mind me asking, how is he… sexually"…

"Gurrrl. Whew! Now that's where William really earns his keep!"

They both burst out laughing when Sheila said that. Annelle wanted to know more and she prodded Sheila for more details because she was interested in knowing if William ever scared her.

"Yeah, most women are satisfied with their HB that way. Has he ever uh… malfunctioned or anything?"

"Not really, I mean, he still isn't completely like having a real man, but he's certainly better than a vibrator", she laughed. "He does what I ask, and I had to get used to asking… you know what I mean? A couple of times over the years, he got stalled, and I found him in his room and it was scary because he was sitting there, not moving, not responding to my calling him. I called the technicians and they eventually came to do some kind of reset. But that only happened like twice. I did receive a couple of upgrades and he gets his regular maintenance that comes with the lifetime warranty… Oh lord, here comes Stacey…"

"Oh shit…. Here she comes. I knew that nosey bitch would eventually make her way out here" Annelle exclaimed. She was semi-annoyed, but she kind of expected the intrusion.

Sheila laughed… "Y'all have been friends for a long time, right?"

"Yeah….. We grew up together… me, her, and Janice. And it's more like a 'love-hate' relationship. She's like a sister who you love, but she gets on your nerves a lot, you know? She has issues herself as it is, but she lives in denial, and constantly compares herself to others as if that gives her life some kind of validation. It's so sad, really to see her not allow herself to be truly happy with herself. She is the ultimate drama queen and lives to be difficult, as you have probably already noticed."

"Yep. I have certainly noticed… Hi Stacey… tired of the band in there?"

"Hey y'all. Yeah… I've had enough of that country music. I figured I'd come out here and relax with y'all…"

"Well I was just about to leave actually" Sheila said as she leaned forward in her seat to stretch and yawn. "I am so tired and I want to get a good night's sleep before that horseback riding tour tomorrow. Are you coming on the tour?"

"Yeah, I'm coming… You going up to your room too, Annelle?"

"No, I'll sit out here with you for a little while. Is Janice, Candace and Pat still in the lounge?"

"Janice went up to your room to go to bed, but Candace and Patlyn were still there when I walked out."

So they sat in the lounge chairs for a while, not saying much, looking up into the beautiful night sky, seeing stars, which was something to behold after years of cloudiness that resulted from the nuclear event. After about twenty minutes, Stacey woke up and tapped Annelle's arm, as they had both nodded out and they both went up to their rooms to bed.

The next morning, they all got up to do the horseback riding tour that took them through some magnificent river canyons and such serene trails. The tour guide pointed out structures that were sculpted into the mountain rock that were named and are well known landmarks, as well as some of the wildlife that they would expect to see and some of the indigenous cactus and plant life that was still around, having survived the change in climate and atmosphere after the nuclear event. Even Stacey enjoyed herself, which surprised all of them. And although Sheila was afraid at first, she rode her horse like a champ and once the tour was over, they were in a very good mood, feeling grateful and fortunate. The following days they all did the yoga sessions, shopping, visiting museums and art galleries, as well as some spa treatments, which ended with all of them getting a hot stone massage and facials.

5 THE GETAWAY – HOMEWARD BOUND

"I hate to leave this place. Can't we stay another week?" Annelle was not ready to go and Janice laughed at her question about staying because it was so hard to get Annelle to go in the first place. They all had lunch together and then boarded the spa resort's shuttle to head for the airport. They all hugged as they got out of the airport shuttle from the spa resort and promised to plan to get together that way again. Annelle and Janice boarded the plane to return to Indiana and as soon as Annelle buckled her seat belt, she began to reflect on the past week, how therapeutic it was for her, and how calm she felt. Without a doubt, the trip was exactly what she needed. She sat in her seat by the window, which was her usual request because no matter how much she has flown, she still liked to gaze out of the window of the plane while flying. She would never drink much beverage, and make sure she emptied her bladder right before boarding so that she wouldn't have to use the nasty airplane restroom that seemed to always be pissed up by people missing the bowl and dripping some on the floor, making it sticky. More often than not, she would seem to end up sitting directly over the wing for some reason. By the time her plane took off, it was approaching evening time and getting dark outside. Since she was flying east, it seemed like they were flying into the darkness and the wing light was illuminating off and on as usual. And, as usual, the thought popped into her head of the 'little monster' sitting out there on the wing. She laughed to herself at that thought that always popped into her head when flying at night if she was sitting over the wing, and she blamed her aunt for it. She promised herself that she would call her aunt once she got home. She was just amazed at how those visits to her aunt's house during some holidays where they would always end up seeing some very old re-runs of an old TV show called *The Twilight Zone*, stuck in her head. It was perplexing to Annelle that such a thing seemed to come to mind, every time, and she laughed to herself about it. She managed to drift off to sleep, although there was literally no way to be comfortable in coach, so that meant to her that she was really tired. She woke up as the steward announced that they would be collecting all trash as they were approaching their destination, and would soon need to be putting their tray tables up, and fastening their seat belts. As they began their descent, Annelle felt some of the issues she left at home before her vacation seep back into her brain. She allowed them to slowly creep in and seemed to revert back to reassuring herself that she deserved that vacation even though the plane hadn't even landed yet. She was thinking about how glad she was after all, that she was fired from Nibiodymics. She thought about how hard it was to go on vacations and how insulted she was when Walter had the nerve to ask her to cancel her vacation two days after giving her a bonus one time. There was no respect anymore and everyone felt that people would just accept any abuse just to have a job. Well, she probably would still be accepting the abuse had they not let her go. She found it incredibly appalling that corporations had ditched all morals and ethics in regard to quality and commitment to service behind their greed to make more and more profit. Her warnings and raising issues that cost money for defects were just not in line with the attitude they wanted around anymore. And if she could ever prove it, she still had the nagging suspicion that Ted was going to kill her and she never got the chance to do the analysis to find out how he was programmed. That, had to be on purpose she felt, and decided that she was going to somehow continue trying to find out what really happened. And the more she thought about all that, the more she knew she couldn't just let it go. She decided that once she got home, she will call Bruce because he understood a lot about the dynamics of corporations and was cynical enough to see where she was coming from. Out of all of her friends, he was the only one who even considered that she could possibly be right in some way about Ted. The more she thought about it, she knew it was best to confide in Bruce because like most real men, he hated HBs. He hated them like most men who weren't making money in some way, off of them, although some men who were profiting from HBs, didn't like them either. However, greed and money made it a necessary evil.

Janice was already off the plane by the time Annelle was able to get out since she was sitting a few rows ahead of her. They had separate modes of transportation to get home since they lived in opposite directions from the airport. They said their goodbyes and once Annelle finally got home, she felt glad to be in her familiar place even after a glorious vacation. *Nothing like sleeping in your own bed* she thought and she flopped down onto her living room couch. She looked at her luggage and decided to leave it right where it was, in the middle of the floor. After sitting for a few moments, she got up and went up to her bedroom and went to bed, thinking about how she would call her aunt first thing in the morning, and then call Bruce to let both of them know she was back.

She slept well into the morning and awoke, startled for some reason. She sat up and looked around and thought she might still be feeling effects of Ted. And although months had gone by, she still sometimes missed him, oddly enough. She put the thought away, and began thinking about what she planned to do that day and going forward because she needed to gather more information to include in her proposal. She had been gone for a week and was surprised that she managed to relax and put her work aside, which was the goal. Now she felt refreshed and renewed with energy to move forward. Reaching for the phone, she saw that she had some messages waiting but decided to call her aunt before listening to them.

"Hi Aunt Cydney! I'm back from my trip."

"Oh Hi baby! I thought you might be back by now. How was your trip? I bet it was beautiful out there."

"Yes it was. I really needed a vacation and Janice set up an agenda for us and it was perfect. We did Yoga and Horseback Riding and I took lots of pictures, so I'll bring them with me when I come down for Thanksgiving. I thought I might try and go through some of the stuff we put in your garage after my parents' passed away to help you get rid of it while I'm there. We can probably give a lot of it to one of your local charities or your church…"

"Wellllll… we don't have to be worrying about that stuff, it's not in my way…"

Just then, Annelle heard her doorbell ring and she jumped up while still talking to her Aunt and ran to her closet for her robe. She skipped down the stairs and looked out the peep hole and saw Bruce standing there.

"Hold on Aunt Cydney. Bruce! Come in! I was gonna call you as soon as I got off the phone with Aunt Cydney."

"Hey girl! I knew you were back and I was already out so I wanted to bring this pile of mail over to you that I collected for you all week."

He walked in after hugging her and went into her dining room to put her bag of mail on the table as she continued to talk to her Aunt for a few more moments.

"Aunt Cydney, I thought you said you wanted to clean out that garage and try to see if your Gremlin still runs…"

"I know, I know… I am planning to go through that stuff and by the time you get down here, I'll probably have my Gremlin on the road."

They both laughed at that because Aunt Cydney had been saying that same thing for years.

"You are welcome to bring your friends for Thanksgiving… you know that. I can't wait to see you. Oh, by the way, I saw a report on the news that there have been some problems with those HBs…"

"On the news?"

" Yes. And seems like the media is trying to downplay the problems that have occurred. I knew you were right about them. I'm so glad you left that company…"

"I didn't leave Aunt Cydney… they fired me. But I'm going to try and get back in, with a proposal for a new design. I'll talk about it more with you later, Aunt Cydney…"

"Oh OK. Tell Bruce I said Hello. Have a blessed day honey."

"OK. You too Aunt Cydney… bye."

Annelle turned to Bruce who had gone into her kitchen and got himself a bottle of water and come back into the living room and sat down. Before she could even open her mouth he said…

"Wait. What the hell is a Gremlin?"

She laughed out loud at him because he was truly puzzled and had a perplexed look on his face.

"No really. What is it? Don't tell me… you've hid another robot in your Aunt's garage. What does this one do? Gremlin? Wow. That doesn't sound good though. What is it… some kind of home security demon?"

Annelle was still laughing as Bruce went on.

"Stop it Bruce, you got me dying laughing! It's a car!"

"A car? I've never heard of that car before."

"Yeah well, Aunt Cydney keeps everything. She actually has her 1974 Green Gremlin in her garage, and last time I was there, the damn thing actually started up. She keeps saying that she wants to get it restored so she can drive it again. It's the ugliest car I have ever seen." They both laughed as Annelle went on…

"There's no way she will be able to get that old thing on the road again with all the environmental regulations that have happened since then. At best, she might be able to get historical plates and register it so that she can take it for a spin on special occasions. I'll make sure you see it if you come with me Thanksgiving. I haven't been down to Georgia in years and I promised Aunt Cydney that I'd spend it with her this year. You're invited, of course. We have a great time because we cook all the foods we love, with all the butter and creams and cheeses with reckless abandon! We watch what we eat all year long, so Thanksgiving… we just let go and let live. Ummmm… My mouth waters just thinking about it. And if we survive dinner without having a cholesterol heart attack, we sit down to watch some of her old DVDs like The Twilight Zone, Andy Griffith, Martin, The Cosbys, The Three Stooges…"

"Wow. Man, it's amazing that that stuff is still funny. I remember my parents watching those marathons years ago during the holidays too. I think I might take you up on that invitation, Annelle. I thought I might try to get my brother and sister to come to Hammond but I've changed my mind. Now, have you downloaded your pictures yet? Let's watch them on your big screen TV."

"Good idea. How's your brother anyway? I think I might want to talk to him because you know I'm working on a proposal and I'm planning on presenting it to Walter, but I want to come up with a new software design that can be patented, and used in HBs. I want to do it as my own company possibly or with another company, but I need some legal advice…"

"Well, he finally got himself together and to tell you the truth, he has joined one of those groups that are protesting the creation of HBs. So he may not be the best person to talk to."

"But he might like my idea because I'm working on changing the purpose of HBs, to make them more generic and actual home assistants rather than female companions…"

"I think that is an excellent idea Annelle. Now can we please look at the pictures? I want to see the beautiful landscape…"

ABOUT THE AUTHOR

Cyd Webster is an IT professional for over 27 years but writing has been her passion since childhood. She is a life-long resident in New Jersey, with a short four year stay in Columbus, Ohio where she graduated from The Ohio State University with a Bachelor degree. She loves to travel and has visited many cities throughout the United States, provinces in Canada, Mexico, countries in Central America, South America, Europe, and the Middle East.

HB is Cyd's first novel which promises to be a thriller that will keep the reader on edge in a story that tackles tough issues in our society. Using a prophetic premise, the story explores a possible future in response to nuclear devastation. *HB – The Getaway - Chapter 5* is an excerpt from the novel *HB,* and has become popular among many women who have read the entire book. She is also author of *Struck by Lightning and other bolts of reality*, a collection of tragic short stories about dysfunctional relationships.

Thankful, grateful and blessed is how she describes herself and her motto is 'Happiness is a choice!'

www.cydwebster.com

www.ingramcontent.com/pod-product-compliance
Lightning Source LLC
Chambersburg PA
CBHW071211130626
46555CB00004B/1671